# The Unveiling of Amber

## Viola Russell

ISBN 978-1-912768-68-4

Published 2019

Published by Black Velvet Seductions Publishing

The Unveiling of Amber Copyright 2019 Viola Russell
Cover design Copyright 2019 Jessica Greeley

Visit us at:
www.blackvelvetseductions.com

For my husband Ben, my inspiration

# Chapter One

## August 1997

ABC News anchor:

*Musician Lucien Travis has died! The guitarist's Mercedes was found at the bottom of a ravine in the Texas town of Spring. Forty-year-old Travis was on his way to an appearance on Austin City Limits and never made it to the performance. His manager, Terry Page, discovered the crash after she traced his route to the performance. The vehicle was at the bottom of the ravine. Travis's body has not been found. This tragedy comes only two months after Travis's wife, Delta, died mysteriously in their home. The couple's young son Justin discovered his mother's body, and the incident is under investigation.*

## New Orleans, November 2017

"What's wrong? You seem distant." Amber ran a hand lightly over her boyfriend's forearm. She could feel his muscles tighten under her touch, and she moved closer to him, drinking in his masculinity. They were alone in his shotgun double in Uptown New Orleans on a cold winter night. They sat on the sofa together, sipping wine and munching on cheese.

"Look, this isn't easy." Tyler turned to her, his mouth set in a firm line. Her arm was linked in his. He'd poured a glass of wine for her and himself. Setting the wine aside, he said, "I've been rehearsing this in my mind for a long time."

*Maybe he's going to ask me to marry him.* The thought raced through Amber's mind, leaving her with a tingling sensation. She leaned closer to him, running her lips along his cheek. He flinched and rose abruptly from his seat beside her.

Tyler ran a hand through his hair. God, how Amber loved that dark hair! It was thick and black. When he looked at her with those startling green eyes, Amber's heart skipped a beat. Of course, none of her colleagues at her conservative local Catholic school even knew she had a boyfriend, and they certainly didn't think she possessed lustful thoughts. School librarians kept students quiet and doggedly guarded the books. *Never mind that she introduced innovative techniques and policies . . . Oh, well.*

Tyler paced the carpet in front of her, fisting and then unclenching his hands. "I've had something to tell you for a long time."

At that moment, the door swung open, and Adrienne, Amber's best friend, strode inside and turned to close the door behind her. She'd barely stepped inside before she turned, obscuring them from her line of vision.

"Hey, Tyler honey, did you tell her? I can't stand the secrecy, and—"

She stopped abruptly, turning and suddenly seeing Amber with Tyler.

*Adrienne had a key to his apartment? Amber had a key as well. Did he simply give his keys to random women? And what the hell did Adrienne mean?* An uneasy feeling developed in Amber's stomach. She threw a confused look in Tyler's direction. He'd gone white, his fists still clenching and unclenching at his side. He was clearly debating what to do.

Amber swallowed and found her voice. "What in hell is going on here?"

Adrienne approached her mouth a round O. She was in shorts that showed the cheeks of her butt; the tank top she wore showed her nipples. Never had Amber seen her religion teacher friend dressed like this. Never.

Adrienne's mouth moved feebly before she finally said, "We've been together for some time, Amber."

The words echoed in Amber's brain. Only a few days ago, she'd lain in Tyler's bed and reveled in the warmth of his arms. His embrace had been pure sensuality. No, this couldn't be happening.

Amber turned to Tyler, who remained silent, and pushed his arm away. She fought back angry and hurt tears. "When were you going to tell me, Tyler? When?"

Tyler started to speak. His mouth moved, but he stayed silent. He stood, turned on his heel, and disappeared into the kitchen.

Amber then turned to Adrienne. "You do realize he was with me only a few days ago, don't you? Did you think we weren't having sex?"

Adrienne stared at her for a long time. She placed her purse on the sofa and said evenly, patronizingly, "Look, Tyler and I just love each other." Her voice took on a gushing tone. "We fulfill each other in soul and body in ways that you and he don't. He said you were too virginal to fulfill him."

Amber blinked away tears and laughed bitterly. "Is that what he's told you? Funny, considering we do everything." She strode into the kitchen.

Tyler was rummaging through the refrigerator and slammed it shut when she entered. Adrienne was on his heels.

"Shit, Adrienne, I told you not to come tonight." He held a container of potato salad in his hand but still looked ashen. "You ruined everything."

Adrienne stared at him with wide eyes. "*I* ruined everything? You told me your relationship with Amber was non-existent. You said she was like ice, like a stone. You called her Sister Mary Margaret."

Amber's shocked gaze drifted from her once-adored boyfriend to her once-loyal friend. "Adrienne, why did you believe him? And Tyler, how could you tell anyone that when you know how crazy we can be?"

Tyler hurled the container into the sink. "You two took this shit too seriously, for fuck's sake. What did you think? I wasn't proposing marriage. I gotta eat dinner. If you'd like to join me and make a—"

"Screw you!" Adrienne's face crumpled into tears, and she sprinted from the kitchen. Amber heard the door slam hard and then Adrienne shouting. "I—I don't need you! I'm pretty. People say I'm like Snow White. My prince will kiss me awake."

Amber almost laughed. *How could the spoiled little bitch say such a thing? Well, her daddy was some wealthy executive. She'd always been taken care of in a material way.*

"Well, I guess it's still us." Tyler turned to open the fridge again.

*How could she ever have been attracted to such a callous dope?* Amber fought the tears threatening to blind her. She wasn't sure if they came from anger or grief. She'd loved this guy, and not only had he betrayed her, he was showing himself to be a royal asshole. How could she have been so blinded?

"No, Tyler, don't be an idiot. It's not *us*. Stay away from me."

"Look, shit happens." He shrugged and tossed the container into a nearby garbage can. "Why do you chicks take everything so seriously? I thought we were all having fun."

"How the hell old are you? Haven't you gained any integrity or sense over the years? Look, at what—twenty-seven—you should have some goddamned sense." Amber blinked back angry tears.

"You suddenly get integrity? You and your friend, that perky religion teacher? I didn't hear any complaints when you groaned like some animal." Tyler leered at her, walked to his refrigerator, cracked open a cheap beer, and took a deep swallow. He sent a mischievous wink her way.

Amber turned on her heel, made her way to the living room, and retrieved her purse and jacket before bolting out the door.

The crisp November air grasped her like the bite of a jungle cat. She turned up her collar and raced down the sidewalk to her car. She stumbled on her own heels and fell against an oak tree. Sobbing, she leaned against the tree until her tears subsided. The old oak felt stable, reliable, and comforting against her back. Apparently, neither her friend nor her lover had her back. Amber was going home to her corgi mix. Apparently, little Alwena was the only one who wouldn't let her down.

### Sunday, two days later

Amber was grateful that she had two days to grieve the loss of Tyler. She'd loved him, or had thought she did. How could she have been so stupid? How could she have befriended a backstabber like Adrienne? When Adrienne had arrived at the school, Amber had shown her the school's proverbial ropes. They had enjoyed many of the same movies and books and had become close confidantes. Now, Amber simply felt like a fool.

She was sitting on her old sofa stroking Alwena while she munched on popcorn. It was then that her phone rang.

Did her mother have some power to let her know when Amber needed to hear her voice?

"Hi, honey, I wanted to know if you were coming to Austin for your grandmother's birthday. Getting away from your job might be hard, but she is getting up in years. Since your dad died, we're all she has."

Vanessa Thorpe had been devoted to her husband, Amber's father. Even when he returned from Iraq as a broken man, she'd stood by him. John Thorpe had never directed his violence against his wife and daughter, but he'd engaged in a number of self-destructive behaviors that had caused them much grief. He'd enjoyed fast motorcycles and too much liquor. His excesses had even dimmed his musical ability. He'd been a multi-instrumentalist before war had taken its toll.

Amber knew her mother never understood why he'd joined the air force during the Gulf War, but strangely, Amber did. Her father was a native-born Texan and infused with patriotism from his own military father. He'd loved his job teaching music, and his music store, but September 11 had inflamed his patriotic spirit. He hadn't died at war, but he'd returned as one of the damaged ones. When he died in a motorcycle accident in his adopted home of New Orleans, police suspected his accident had been purposeful.

Grandma Margaret had adored her son. She was a spunky native Texan who still wore cowboy boots at seventy-seven and lived in suburban Austin. She respected Vanessa's devotion to her son and adored his only daughter.

Vanessa's mother had died when Amber was a teen, and Margaret was now her only grandmother. Of course she would go to Texas, but she sure as hell wouldn't tell Vanessa or Margaret about the humiliating scene with Tyler—not yet. Her mother hadn't liked the bum. She didn't feel like hearing her mother's "I told you so." Any sympathy would have been like burning acid on her soul.

Amber barely kept her voice even. "Sure, I could swing a weekend, but it can't be a long weekend. That skinny bitch principal we have doesn't like it. She even makes us provide pictures of road accidents when we are late by a few minutes. Besides, I have to make provision for Alwena, make a reservation at the boarder's, you know."

"Don't worry, Alwena will be fine. You worry about her like a child. Besides, you need a new job, darling. That woman harasses you too much. When I get back into town, I'll give that skinny Trish Baumann a piece of my mind. The woman is a Nazi." Vanessa was an alumnus of the school but bore it no special love. She hesitated. "What is it, Amber? Something's wrong, I can tell."

Tears flowed before Amber could blink them away. She hadn't intended to say anything. How could her mother's sympathy make her break her own vow so easily? "Mama, he broke up with me. Or, I did with him, and it was because he was sleeping with that bitch Adrienne!"

"That bitch! She's your friend!" Vanessa's horror resonated over the phone.

"I thought so, too." Amber suppressed a sob.

"Take a few days. Tell the bitch Baumann you're sick. Come visit with your grandmother and me."

"Yes, Mama."

Amber pushed a button on the remote. A juicy but predictable mystery flashed on the screen. She didn't know how drastically her life would change on Monday.

# Chapter Two

Amber placed a determined smile on her face as she entered the building on Monday. St. Elizabeth of Hungary was a Catholic co-ed school that catered to the city's supposedly devout. In reality, most of the residents used it as a means of isolating their children from those they considered unsavory elements.

Amber hadn't liked the school when she'd attended it, but St. Elizabeth had offered her a job upon graduating. She'd grown comfortable and stayed even after earning her master's in library science. Instinctively, Amber knew she'd regret that decision.

At least very few people knew about Tyler, except Adrienne—who she'd thought was a friend. With the advent of social media, Amber knew better than to reveal too much about herself to many of her colleagues, but she cursed herself for so misjudging Adrienne.

Amber wrapped herself in her leather jacket. It was a blustery morning in New Orleans, threatening rain. A streetcar rattled down the road. Tourists and college students made their way to nearby campuses and museums. A streak of lightning illuminated the dark sky, followed by a crash of thunder.

A chill raced through Amber as she made her way inside the school, and a black sense of foreboding cascaded over her like a waterfall.

"Amber, honey, Mrs. Baumann wants to see you." Brenda LeBlanc, the elderly secretary, looked out from her small office as Amber signed in and cast a sympathetic glance her way. "She says it's important."

Amber nodded and then knocked on Trish Baumann's door. What would the woman be on about today? She pinched the budget like no principal Amber had ever known and constantly questioned Amber's every purchase for the library.

"Come in." Trish's high-pitched, whiny voice echoed from the depths of her office. Amber opened the door and entered the room.

She sat behind a huge mahogany desk that made her look like a child playing executive. Her mousy blond hair hung loosely around her face, and her thin hands clutched a pen. Several folders lay on her desk, and a laptop lay open before her. The technical support leader, also a teacher, stood at Trish's side.

Trish indicated the chair across from her desk. She cleared her throat and frowned, seemingly pained or disgusted. Trish was perhaps forty, but her sharp features gave her the appearance of someone fifty or older.

"Something was brought to our attention by a parent, one of our major contributors."

Amber stood ramrod straight, not acknowledging the chair offered her. She couldn't imagine why Trish wanted to see her, but she knew that the principal frequently called people into her office like this before firing them.

Shana Banko, the technical support teacher, took over. She said coldly, "One of our parents came across something involving you online. It seems it has gone viral among the students." She raised her eyebrows and widened her pig-like eyes.

She was as fat as Trish was skinny, with folds around her midsection that protruded from her too-tight blouse. A rotund stomach pressed against a pair of jeans that threatened to bust a button. Flabby arms and chubby fingers worked at the laptop on the principal's desk.

"I've never published a thing online." Amber looked from one woman to the other, genuinely confused. Still, a sinking feeling formed at the pit of her stomach. Where was this going?

Shana's gaze narrowed further. "You and Ms. Adrienne Torelli apparently have a mutual friend."

Okay, so they knew about Tyler. Well, how was it anyone's business, and what in hell did this have to do with some video? "I don't understand."

Trish glanced up at her compatriot, looking grimly smug. "Show her."

Shana turned the computer so that the screen faced Amber. The image of Amber herself engaged in a very sensual moment with Tyler loomed on the screen. Their bodies were bare and locked together in an embrace of heated passion. He was nibbling on her neck and then her breasts. Then, she took him in her mouth. Amber sank down heavily in the chair across from Trish. The breath left her body. She'd never known Tyler, the asshole, had filmed their most intimate moments. Jesus!

"This is a Catholic school. We can't have this behavior for our children to see." Trish folded her hands on her desk, the pen falling from her grip. She looked smugly satisfied. Amber wondered if the woman always wore blouses with Peter Pan collars. How prim did she need to look? "Too many of them have seen it already. They may be damaged for life. Parents want your immediate dismissal."

Amber swallowed hard. She wouldn't cry. Her grandmother had taught her never to show weakness, but she knew her cheeks were burning bright. "I never knew about those videos."

Trish glanced at Shana, clasped her own hands even tighter, and said coldly, "That may be the case, but it is irrelevant. We have impressionable teenagers here. Our parents expect something different. We can't have this."

Well, what else could the woman say? Amber actually understood their position, but she hated the smug way they looked at each other.

Trish had gone to school with Amber's mother. Vanessa had always been the popular, beautiful girl who wore outlandish earrings and often visited the disciplinarian's office but was still loved by all. Administrators had smiled indulgently at her foibles as childish mischief, and her parents, though not wealthy, had adored her and her younger brother. Trish had been the homely outcast whose military father had drunk himself to death and whose mother had put a bullet through her head. After their deaths, her grandmother had taken her in but had required her to perform hours of housework. Trish hated girls like Vanessa and her daughter.

Amber managed to match Trish's smug smile. "I completely understand, but I want to say this first." When Shana started to open her mouth, Amber shot her a look of such ferocity that the woman immediately clamped her mouth shut. "You and your minions have terrorized anyone who was in this school before you came or who had any allegiance to the old administration." She turned to Shana. "You, for example, said you thought one teacher didn't know what plagiarism was. Well, she has a doctorate, so I guess she does understand that, you fat fuck."

Shana emitted an outraged gasp and turned to Trish, who was reaching for her phone. The "O" that Shana's mouth formed made her look like a huge doughnut. "Are you going to—?"

"Oh, come on, Trish. I'll go. You don't have to call the police." Amber laughed. They were afraid of her. The absurdity of the situation struck her like a pleasurable sexual current. "Before I go, I also want to say to you, you skinny bitch, that the email criticizing my filing system was unprofessional and inaccurate. Nothing was wrong with the system, and when you ever criticize an employee, you don't send it to the whole school." Hot coals raced through Amber as she remembered the incident. "Oh, by the way, I know you didn't like my email response, but Trish, it's not my fault that your parents didn't love you." Amber had made delightful use of Trish's family history in her response.

Trish went white. Her hands were clasped together so tightly that the knuckles formed very pale mini-fists all their own. Every vein in her hands showed. "You don't know what you're talking about, and you didn't have to put that in an email."

Amber grinned. "When I brought my complaints to the archdiocese, they agreed with me. They thought your behavior was unprofessional." She laughed dryly and shrugged. "So, I lost today. I won't in the future."

With those words, she rose from her seat, turned on her heel, and slammed the door.

Amber marched out of the building, traversed the schoolyard, and avoided the stares of the arriving students. She threw open the library door, strode to her desk, and thrust the framed portrait of her parents into her purse. As she walked to her car, raindrops began falling. Amber made it to her car, but not before she heard the stifled snickers of several students and noted several boys grabbing their crotches. Was she forever to be a cock joke for teenaged boys?

***

Tyler the sonofabitch! Amber wondered if she could have the videos taken down. Still, too many who knew her had already seen them.

Her friends began calling soon after her dismissal. Well, at least she wasn't the only one in disgrace. The little bitch Adrienne had also had her nude body exposed all over the Internet.

Amber wondered how she could face Vanessa and Margaret in Austin. She prayed her mother and grandmother hadn't heard of her indiscretions and stupidity; however, she also wanted her mother's advice and comfort. Why was it that she still needed her mother's warm hands—even as a grown woman? Maybe no one ever stopped needing that love.

After depositing a pouting Alwena at the boarder's and placing a kiss on the dog's head, Amber made her way to the airport.

Vanessa and Margaret met her in Austin. As usual, Margaret wore her staple cowboy boots and denim blouse. She looked chic in the fur coat that protected her from the brisk wind. Though in her seventies, Margaret still dyed her hair the flaming red of her youth.

Smiling broadly, she waved at Amber and enfolded her in a long embrace. "My precious girl, give Gran a kiss and let me look at you."

The warm greeting sent a wave of love mingled with sadness through Amber's whole psyche. She quickly blinked away the tears that sprang to her eyes, swallowed, and forced a smile when Margaret held her at arm's length.

Vanessa, looking gorgeous in a denim jacket, embraced her next and looked at Amber searchingly. Amber always felt that she was like a dull spark compared to her mother's soaring beauty. While Amber's hair was a dark auburn, Vanessa had shining blond hair that made men turn their heads. While Amber had to work hard to maintain her figure, her mother was naturally svelte but curvy. Though in her fifties, Vanessa attracted the attention of men half her age. Her smile dazzled with a genuine love of life that infected all who met her. Still, Amber knew the deep sadness her mother harbored since the death of her husband.

They had once been part of a wide circle of friends and couples that Vanessa had discarded when Amber was young. When Amber had once asked about where their friends went and why her parents had put aside a lifetime of travel and parties, Vanessa had simply said, "That life is over." Since John's death, Vanessa had met no one special. She saw men occasionally, but they failed to arouse her interest.

She'd immersed herself in cultivating Amber. There had been guitar lessons, dancing lessons, and swimming lessons. Amber had gone to good schools and studied writing at an exclusive arts school.

Vanessa walked beside Amber as they made the trek to baggage claim. "Is something else bothering you beside that jerk Tyler?"

"Not in front of Gran Margaret." Amber shook her head in warning as Margaret turned to them. Amber smiled at her grandmother.

Margaret gave her a searching look but said nothing.

As Amber unpacked her clothes in her grandmother's house, she reflected on her next move. She couldn't hide the truth forever. Vanessa knew her too well, and her grandmother was too astute. She sighed heavily and sat on the bed.

The tears came in the form of heavy sobs. Within a few days, she'd lost everything—her boyfriend, her job, her friend, and her credibility. Amber had thought she loved Tyler. Apparently, he hadn't felt the same, and not only had he not reciprocated her love, he'd betrayed her with a metaphoric blow to the gut, making certain her life would be changed forever. She'd thought Adrienne was a friend, but this friend had slept with her boyfriend and then played an innocent when she'd been revealed. But, Amber had practical issues to consider. She would need a job soon, or she wouldn't be able to afford even her small Mid-City apartment. *How would she feed Alwena? She couldn't lose her baby!*

As if on cue, Vanessa pushed open the door. "I thought you might need help unpacking, and now I hear you crying." She sat beside Amber on the bed and took her face in her hands. "Tell me what's wrong. Tyler's one jerk. Why has this hurt you so much?"

"Mom, you don't know the half of it. It's much worse than his breaking up with me. He—he—"

The words spilled from Amber. She revealed every detail of the past few days, ending with "He'd taken videos of us, Mom. He put them online for the whole damned world to see."

"Amber, how could you let him film you? You know better." Vanessa shook her head, disbelieving.

"I didn't know he was filming us. I swear I didn't. Hell, I don't know why he's so bitter or wants to ruin me. Then, that bitch Baumann fired me."

"Bitch is right!" Vanessa's lips formed a thin line. "Well, I'm not surprised about her. She always loved condemning anyone who had better sex than she did."

Amber laughed in spite of her tears. Vanessa could always make her laugh, but her mother's flippant comment disarmed her. She hadn't completely horrified or scandalized her mother.

"Don't hate me," she said.

Vanessa drew her into her arms. "You know better than that. I'd never hate you, and if you say you didn't know about his devious actions, then you're a victim. My love, stay here for a while." Vanessa's lips brushed Amber's hair. "I don't have to be back in New Orleans soon, either. We can hang with your grandmother. Shop. We'll come up with a game plan."

"Okay, just don't say anything to Gran right now." Amber met her mother's gaze. "Please, Mom. I don't know how I'll ever face her if she knows." A twinge of guilt tugged at Amber's heart. She suddenly felt very lonely. "I can't stay too long, though. I miss Alwena when she's at the boarder's."

"Okay, but don't worry about money. You can always move in with me if you need to, hon." Vanessa embraced her tighter.

"I know, but I need to decide my next move for myself." Amber wouldn't rely on anyone anymore, not even her mother.

# Chapter Three

Margaret's party was on a Sunday, and Vanessa packed several adventures into the week leading up to it. Amber was amazed at her grandmother's stamina as she traveled with them from shopping malls, to museums, to music venues.

Margaret donned her cowboy boots and insisted that Amber and Vanessa wear them as well. The Friday before the party, Amber accompanied them to Friends, a blues venue on Sixth Street.

Amber wore her "Keep Austin Weird" T-shirt under her leather jacket, and black feather earrings. She enjoyed the vibe of Austin nightlife and settled into her place at the table with a rum and coke. Several men cast glances in their direction, but Amber doubted that their looks were meant for her. Her mother looked fetching in a jean skirt and cherry red sweater, and her grandmother glowed in jeans that accented her still-shapely figure. Well, Amber was content to be the wallflower in the trio. She'd had enough of men for the moment and was more than happy to sip her drink in peace.

A young man in a huge cowboy hat and sunglasses extended a gentlemanly hand to Margaret, who flashed the Texan a flirtatious smile and let him lead her onto the floor while the band played a haunting blues tune, the harmonica wailing a plaintive cry of loss and angst. Amber grinned as her grandmother swayed against the man young enough to be her grandson.

Another man winked at Vanessa and strode over to lead her to the floor. Amber wondered if she was emitting a vibe that was scaring men away. If she was, she was glad.

Amber watched the crowd sway to the music as it swelled into a crescendo of sound that sent her pulse racing. She loved music, loved the sound, loved the vibrations, and loved the way it made her feel.

The band paused after the song, imbibing the beers an admirer had purchased for them. It was then that she noticed him. A man approached the stage, talking to the band. They nodded, apparently intrigued by the stranger's proposal.

He was tall and wonderfully thin. He wore a black cowboy hat not unlike that worn by many of the men in the establishment, but it was filled with pins symbolizing things that must have held personal significance for him. One she recognized as a medal for valor. The other was a glaringly scary skull. What struck Amber, however, was his face. He was so scarred that she couldn't determine his age, or even his race for certain. Only his strikingly thin hands betrayed him as white. Deep crevices marked his cheeks and brow; scars intermingled with those craters to produce a haunting image of some phantom from a medieval tale. When the band resumed, the man had strapped on a guitar and joined them.

Amber sat enraptured as this scarred figure produced soaring chords from the guitar. She'd never heard anything like it—not in her experience listening to the grunge bands of her youth or the punk music she'd adopted as a nod to nostalgia. No, this kind of voodoo on a guitar she'd never heard. Her father had been amazing, but this was beyond what any human could do.

"Who is that guy?" Margaret stared at the man and looked from Vanessa to Amber. She'd left her young dance partner with a wink and pat on the rump.

"I don't know, but I've never heard of anyone like him since the 1960s or □70s." Vanessa returned to her seat with a drink in hand, compliments of her dance partner who still stared at her from across the room. She stared into the distance as if remembering something.

"The □60s?" Amber raised an eyebrow. She grinned at Vanessa. "You must mean someone specific, Mom."

Vanessa sipped her drink. She looked away and then turned to Amber with a smile that seemed somehow forced. "Lucien Travis, to be precise, but that poor man is long dead. This guy can make that guitar wail just like he could." She added wistfully, "And your dad was great in his day, too, but John really shone on piano. Lucien was a master at the guitar."

Margaret shot Vanessa a glance Amber couldn't read. The elderly woman concentrated on her drink. She said softly, "Yes, the boy had talent. It wasn't as if a human being was playing."

Amber suppressed the sadness that memories of her father could arouse and gazed at the man on stage. He was mesmerizing as he leaned forward, forcing cacophonous but powerful melodies from his instrument. He swayed backward and forward as fingers raced across the fretboard, teasing intoxicating sounds from the guitar with every movement of his fingers. No capo. Only those thin hands with the long, slender fingers.

Amber shook herself slightly to break her own reverie. The man was obviously old enough to be her father—and scarred at that—but he was hypnotic. Never had she heard anyone play like that—not even her father, who could make any instrument sing.

The stranger played for two songs, removed the guitar strap from around his shoulders, gingerly set the instrument aside, and stepped from the stage. The other musicians, obviously much younger, stared in awe. One called after him, "Hey, would you like a regular gig?"

The musician just laughed, a hoarse chuckle. He turned on his heel and stepped outside. Amber could see him as he lit a cigarette and then inhaled deeply. He looked around and then through the window. Was it her imagination or was he really looking at her?

Her mother and grandmother had moved on to other partners. Amber alone was the wallflower. Well, maybe the sourness in her soul had found a home in her face. She certainly didn't feel like a sex magnet. Tyler's behavior still hurt. He and his stupidity had cost her everything, including her own self-respect. How would she ever find a teaching job again? Still, a slowly dawning realization pounded in her consciousness. She couldn't be completely dead inside—the walking wounded or the zombie-propelled dead woman. This intriguing stranger had excited something within her.

Suddenly, Amber lost sight of him, and then, he was at the bar. When he turned, he held two drinks in his hand and was walking toward her. The prospect of talking to this stranger both frightened and titillated her.

"You looked lonely. Those two ladies seem to have found other friends." The Scarred One placed the drinks on the table and sat across from her.

Amber laughed wryly. "Those two ladies are my mother and grandmother. They've had more dances than I have." She looked down and blushed.

"Pretty ladies." He smiled at her and extended a hand. The smile distorted his face even more, but Amber sensed he'd once been a handsome man. Even the touch of his hand was electric. "Winston, Winston Hurley."

"Amber Thorpe." Amber's own voice sounded hollow in her ears. "We're here visiting my grandmother."

"So not a native Texan?" Hurley took a sip of his drink.

"No, my dad was. He died too young." Amber felt her throat grow tight. The memory of her father still hurt.

"Hold onto those good memories." Winston smiled at her. Scars distorted the smile, making him seem otherworldly—almost like a skeleton unevenly decayed. He took another sip of his drink and stared ahead. "Sometimes memories are all we have."

"I wish I'd had him a little longer." Amber swallowed hard. Memories of her father still hurt like a stabbing wound. She especially missed him now. *God, how she needed his advice at this dark time!* She added quickly, hoping to change the somber mood, "I love the way you play. My dad could play, too."

"Well, I've played since I was a kid. Way before you were born, I'm sure." Hurley tipped the hat back, showing a broad and scarred forehead. "Of course, I'm no Stevie Ray or Clapton. I certainly ain't that wizard Jimi Hendrix. Don't pretend to be."

"Are you kidding? You're amazing." Amber felt her face grow hot at her own indiscretion, but she plowed on, even against her better judgment. "I've heard recordings of those other guys, and you're every bit as good."

"Well, darling, you make an old guy happy, but I'm just a picker who first played on a used guitar his daddy had bought from a second-rate store." Hurley shrugged and took another sip from his drink. "It's rare I play like I did today. Since my accident, I don't go out much."

"Oh, I see." Amber looked down and frowned. Why did she have the feeling she'd spoken of things he'd like to forget? She added quickly, "We can talk about something else."

"No, sweetheart, you're not making me uncomfortable." He placed a reassuring hand on hers. "It's just that I've heard those guys. Some of them were real geniuses."

"Then, you are, too." Amber wondered if he thought she was merely throwing empty praise his way. She cleared her throat. "I mean it. I'm not just saying that."

"I know that." The words were matter-of-fact. It was his turn to change the subject. "So, where do you live these days?" Hurley's face creased into that distorted grin.

Amber looked down and felt the blood rush to her face. Ordinarily, his type of scars would make her uncomfortable, but she found him strangely magnetic. "I—I'm from New Orleans. My dad moved there when he married my mother."

"What do you do there?" He took a sip from his drink.

Amber linked her fingers. She bit her lip before answering. "I am— was a librarian."

"Not now?" He studied her, pushing his hat back. Amber saw that his hair was unnaturally black. Well, at least he was smart enough not to make librarian jokes. Amber had heard too many. They all made librarians sound dull or unimaginative.

The question was innocent, but a hole opened in Amber's chest. She said simply, "No, I—I'm taking a break."

"Cool." He stroked the cigarettes in his pocket. "I have a place in New Orleans in the French Quarter. There's a wine tasting at the Emerald Wine Cellar next Thursday. Will you be back home then? I'd like to take you. There's a pop-up restaurant cooking there. I think they're also tasting Buffalo Trace."

Amber's heart beat fast. Why was this man so appealing? He was handsome—scarred, in fact, but she found him fascinating. He was still lean and moved like a young man. Well, she couldn't really tell if he was young or not. The disfiguring lines traversing his face drew her to him rather than repulsed her. Still, she knew nothing about him. Why did she find herself answering in the affirmative? She knew the shop. It was very public and frequented by locals.

"I'd love to go with you. I'll meet you there."

"Well, that's nice, pretty one." He swirled the liquid in his drink. "I'll need your number." He added quickly, "After all, how will I contact you so we can meet?"

*Why was she giving him her cell phone number?* Amber wrote the number on a folded napkin and handed it to him. At that moment, Vanessa and Margaret rejoined them after planting casual kisses on the cheeks of their dance partners.

Vanessa gave Hurley a curious glance. "Aren't you going to introduce us to your friend, honey?"

"Oh, sure, sorry, Mama." Amber shifted in her seat and made the introductions. "We've been talking about guitarists." Amber wasn't about to tell her mother and grandmother that she was meeting this man for wine and food. No, she had to figure him out first, decide why he so drew her in.

"You certainly can play, Mr. Hurley. I haven't heard anyone like you since Lucien Travis." Vanessa smiled broadly, but she studied him intently whenever he turned his attention elsewhere. Of course, Vanessa was discreet. Only Amber noticed her mother's study of Hurley and the way she stiffened, her arms folded tightly along her midsection. She seemed to be searching for something. What?

Hurley seemed to lose color for a moment, but then he quickly smiled and replied. "Lucien had his good points, no doubt, but there were others greater. We lost a true genius when that son of Texas, Stevie Ray, passed on." He cast what seemed like an involuntary glance upward.

"God rest them and keep them." Margaret added automatically. She held out her glass. "Who's up for another round?"

"On me, ladies."

The frivolity lasted into the early hours of the morning. When Amber and her party finally returned home, they were exhausted and prepared for bed. Vanessa observed before she and Amber parted for the night, "There's something about the man that seems very familiar. I can't shake it. He was very nice, but he reminded me—"

She quickly broke off and looked away, evading Amber's gaze.

"I liked him." Amber wasn't sure why she felt so drawn to him, but she couldn't deny the bizarre attraction she felt—a man old enough to be her father, a damaged man at that, a man about whom she knew nothing.

"Just—" Vanessa paused before turning to enter her room.

"Just be careful. There's something unusual about him. I can't put a hand on it."

"Sure, Mom. There's no reason to warn me. He's just some friendly guy who I may see again back home." Amber didn't tell her mother she was meeting him later that week. She merely planted a light kiss on her mother's cheek and pushed open the door to her room.

# Chapter Four

## The week before Thanksgiving

Amber parked her car in the lot of the Emerald Wine Cellar, sliding into one of the few spaces left. People had already gathered for this popular event in the heart of Mid-City. Vendors participating in the farmer's market hawked their goods in the adjoining lot.

The weather had turned warm; Amber had dressed in a becoming jean skirt and silk blouse. She alighted from the car with Alwena in tow and looked for Winston Hurley. He stood on the steps of the building, obviously searching the crowd. Upon seeing her, he waved and strode briskly toward her. Amber smiled, returned his wave, and studied him as he approached. He clearly wasn't young, but he had the body of a runner and was still agile. His signature jeans fit snugly but becomingly.

Hurley placed a light kiss on her lips. Alwena wagged her tail but sniffed him cautiously. Almost involuntarily, Amber slid her arms around his neck. What was his pull on her? Why did the mere touch of his lips send an electric shock through her whole body?

"I'm glad you suggested this."

"Are you now, pretty one? I'm glad you came." He bent to pet Alwena, then slid Amber's arm through his and led her to the young people manning a portable oven. Alwena padded along beside them. "You could have thought I was the bogeyman and run for the hills."

Alwena continued to sniff around his ankles. He grinned at her. "What kind of dog is she? She's sure close to the ground."

"That's my Welsh girl. Her name's Welsh, and she's part corgi. Her daddy was some other indiscriminate breed." Amber winked. "I think he jumped a fence."

Winston grinned. Why did a part of her think there was something strange, mysterious, and frightening about the man? Obviously, he'd had an accident. Many people had accidents, but Amber sensed something else lurked beneath the surface of his injury. Still, she liked him—liked his Texas drawl and his lopsided smile.

The brisk air gripped but invigorated her. A glass of wine and good food was what she needed. "Who are these pop-up guys?"

"Let's ask them."

A young man with long brown locks and a full beard greeted them. "What can I do for you two today?"

"What's good, my man, and what's your restaurant?" Hurley removed a wallet from his back pocket.

Another young man with long dreadlocks and a blood-smeared apron replied, "We're going to open a butcher shop across the street, and you folks want to try that brisket sandwich."

The warmth from the blazing flames of the portable barbecue pit felt comforting as they flickered behind the workers. Amber rubbed her hands together.

"Sounds good." Hurley turned to Amber. "What about you, darling?"

"The red beans look good." Amber was enjoying herself already. This man had a way of relaxing her and letting her forget her troubles.

It was then that she saw the woman. Long blond hair pulled back in a ponytail, she stood in front of a shotgun double, staring at them and holding a professional camera in her hand. Then, she lifted it and aimed it at them.

Amber indicated the blond and said, "I think she's taking pictures of us. Why would she take pictures of us?"

"Damned if I know. I guess having a camera on your phone isn't good enough anymore." Hurley quickly turned away, moving closer to the makeshift kitchen preparing their food. He was now obscured from view.

"Here you go, mon." The guy with the dreads handed them their food.

Amber and Winston made their way into the bar area where other patrons also munched on their food and sipped inviting libations. Alwena followed. The establishment was pet-friendly. She settled at Amber's feet, looking hopefully in the direction of the food.

The rest of the evening was uneventful. Amber sipped wine with Hurley in the bar while they ate. She occasionally gifted Alwena a piece of sausage.

"So you're from Texas?" Amber studied him over her glass.

Hurley shrugged and removed his hat. "I don't stay in one place much. It's good to avoid attachments."

Amber nodded. Sometimes, she felt the same. Without her family and a few close friends, she'd be lost. Funny, she'd thought Adrienne was a friend . . .

"Well, I can see how that would be, but I have family I'm close to."

"Except for one son, most of my family's gone. That's what happens when you live a long time." Hurley took a bite from his sandwich and wiped his mouth with a napkin. "You don't have that problem yet." He leaned back in his chair.

Amber shrugged. "Sometimes, disappearing sounds nice." For the past two weeks, Amber had wished she could wake from a nightmare or hide somewhere until it was over.

"Disappearing has its charms." He looked ahead and seemingly grew thoughtful. "Of course, you can't always stay lost. People have a way of finding you."

Amber forced a smile. "Well, I grew up in New Orleans. My dad liked the music scene here. He traveled to Austin sometimes when he played in a band, but he owned a music shop and taught classes out of it. He taught piano and guitar. That kept him busy."

"Talented man. Sounds like heaven. You must have loved growing up like that." Hurley leaned forward and tented his hands under his chin. He seemed genuinely interested in what she said.

"Well, I adored him." The lump in Amber's throat grew. "When he died, our finances collapsed. All his money was tied up in the business. We lost just about everything, but my mother worked her butt off to keep me in the same Catholic school where she went to school. Money was tight for a long time. Grandma Margaret helped out, so did my mother's parents. Still, my mother felt that running the house was her responsibility. That's when she got her real estate license. She did really well with it."

"So you liked to read and became a librarian." Hurley took a sip of wine, drained his glass, and then poured them both another. He handed Alwena a piece of meat. She wagged her tail appreciatively and gazed at him adoringly.

"It wasn't that simple. I wanted to open my own business, like my dad, but I never had the guts or the capital." Amber swallowed hard. She had loved to read and had wanted to open her own bookstore, but she'd not possessed the funds to strike out on her own. The degree from LSU had provided her with some security, but she'd failed in pursuing her dreams. She rested her elbows on the table and asked, "So what do you do when you're not playing guitar at night?"

"I'm retired, ma'am." He gallantly lifted the hat and tipped it to her. "I was a full-time musician."

"And a Texan." Amber added. "From where in Texas?"

"I don't talk about that much. Don't ask." His voice held an edge, but he quickly smiled and said, "My dad was a preacher. He was pretty strict, and we all had to walk on eggshells. He didn't like that I wanted to be a musician. It was okay when I played in the church choir, but he didn't see being a musician as a real job." He raised an eyebrow and laughed dryly. "The old man also hated the blues, thought of it as Satan's music."

"What did he think of rock 'n' roll?" Amber grinned.

A siren screamed outside. Amber turned to see an ambulance, its lights flashing, racing toward some unknown destination.

"Don't even ask. I won't repeat the things he said in front of a sweet girl like you." Hurley swirled the wine in his glass. He grinned and added dryly, "For all his piety, my old man could have a salty tongue."

"Everyone has a flaw." Amber took a bite of her food.

"Some people aren't just flawed. They're hypocrites." Hurley's tone was bitter. He took a deep swallow of his wine. He added with a shrug, "Of course, I've done some things I regret, too. I guess I shouldn't talk."

Amber shifted uncomfortably in her chair. She sensed she'd ventured onto unwelcome territory. She affected a light tone. "How long will you be in town?"

"Oh, I may stay around. I often play informally at some local clubs." Winston paused. "Some of that depends upon you." He smiled at her.

The casual and friendly dates continued for a week. Amber enjoyed Winston. His humor was wry, and he forced her to forget the troubles that plagued her. She had some money saved, but she knew finding a job after the blow to her reputation would be hard. No school would want to hire the "kinky librarian."

She'd discovered that nickname for her on several social media sites—often posted by students who'd discovered the lascivious video. Although she'd petitioned to have the video removed and had hired a lawyer to help her, Amber soon learned that removing anything from the web was filled with loopholes and bureaucracy.

"You seem down sometimes, Little One? What's going on?" Hurley opened the car door for her after parking in the French Quarter. He took her hand as she stepped onto the sidewalk. Ever the Texas gentleman. The air had again turned brisk. Amber was grateful for her boots and jacket. A sax player plied his trade on the corner. The doleful sounds of his instrument soothed her. The Quarter was quiet on a weeknight. A few tourists gawked in windows of novelty shops. Local kids tap-danced on another corner.

The sensation of his hand over hers felt somehow comforting. Amber shrugged and pressed back the tears pushing against her eyes. "Just poor judgment." She hoped her voice wasn't quivering.

"Tell me about it over dinner." Hurley cupped her chin in his hand. "You don't have to keep a stiff upper lip around me, and I'm a good listener."

They made their way to Tableau, a well-known French Quarter eatery located near Jackson Square and the St. Louis Cathedral. Amber glanced at a tattooed tarot card reader and wondered *I wonder what she would tell me?* The woman glanced over at her and smiled. Amber stared a moment too long and then felt Winston squeeze her hand.

It was while they lingered over wine that Amber told Hurley of her transgressions. Hurley said nothing, made no judgments. He simply sipped his wine while she talked. Amber clutched herself as she spoke, sometimes talking too fast, sometimes wiping a tear that strayed down her cheek.

"I can't imagine what you think of me." She looked down and felt her face grow hot. *Why had she confided in the man?*

"Why would I think anything bad of you?" His slow Texas drawl reminded her of her father. "He was the one filming, not you. You were adults in a relationship. The only one who was underhanded was this rat boyfriend of yours." He placed a hand over hers. "*He* posted something without your permission. *He* cheated on you." Hurley shrugged. "That guy's the asshole who should be throttled, not you. Stop beating yourself up." He added quietly, "Was it enjoyable until your privacy was invaded?"

Amber looked at him. There was no mockery in his tone, nor was there any condemnation. He didn't appear to hold any lascivious intent. She said simply, "I—he was my boyfriend. I thought we were in a caring relationship. Of course, I liked our times together." She studied him over her wine glass.

"Then stop feeling guilty. You're a normal woman with normal needs." Hurley caressed her hand. "Sometimes, we do things that society says are inappropriate, but to me"—he shrugged—"if adults do such things and enjoy them, no one should judge."

"Well, my old administration took a dim view of such things." Amber felt her face grow hot. She looked down at her hands. "They didn't want me around."

"Then they're idiots and hypocrites for treating you that way." Hurley caressed her hand but gingerly drew it away. So careful not to seem ungentlemanly, too possessive.

"The kids had found the site, and they jeered—"

"Kids forget. Things blow over. Your administration didn't give you a chance." Hurley looked at her over his wine glass. "It's their loss."

"Well, I'm the one without a job." Amber suddenly felt lost, panicked. She didn't have unlimited resources.

"You'll find another. Let me help you."

"I—I don't want to impose on anyone or burden them with my problems." Amber stared at her glass. His hand lingered on hers again, but there was something very warm and comforting about Winston Hurley. She added suddenly, blinking back tears, "Then, I forgot to pay my rent. My landlord sent me a nasty note. I may be living with my mother."

Hurley gave her a crooked smile. "You could stay at my French Quarter digs. We could check it out tonight."

Amber's heart fluttered. She stammered. "I—I don't know. I have Alwena."

"I love dogs, and she's a sweet pooch. She's very welcome as well." Winston let her digest his offer.

They finished their meal in congenial silence. After paying the bill, they made their way into Jackson Square.

It was Winston who continued the conversation. "Nothing would happen, pretty one. It's just a friendly offer. I'll show it to you. If you like it, you can stay. I have some gigs in Austin soon. I wouldn't be around much." He reached into his shirt pocket for a cigarette and lit it. The New Orleans air was muggy. He took a long draw and stared into the night. "I'm also looking for some gigs in New Orleans. We'd see each other from time to time, but I'd be happy someone was watching the house."

"I don't have the kind of money to pay for an apartment in the

Quarter." Amber's cheeks grew hot.

Winston led her to a bench. General Jackson and his horse loomed on the horizon. "You'd do me the favor, as I said. You'd look after the place. I can't be there all the time." He crossed one booted foot over his knee.

"So I'd house-sit?"

"You could think of it that way, but I think you should see the house. It's not an apartment, by the way."

The tarot card reader was still there. Amber indicated the woman. "I want to talk to her."

Winston raised a skeptical brow. "Do you believe in that stuff?"

*Did she?* Amber shrugged, stood, and stared in the woman's direction. "Who knows? It may be fun, maybe even illuminating."

Holding Winston's hand, Amber made her way to the woman. This one was younger than some of the others. She also charged less than her counterparts.

Winston handed her the money. "Yeah, it might be fun," he agreed.

The tarot card reader smiled at them. She wore elaborate emerald jewelry that was clearly paste, a flowing black skirt and a puffy white blouse. Her dark hair was pulled back in a scarf marked by a skull and crossbones.

"I'm Eve." She took Amber's hand and turned it over, studying the palm.

"Are you going to tell me I'm going to meet a mysterious stranger?" Amber grinned weakly. Her pulse was throbbing. Why did her own words seem so ominous—even to herself?

Winston had retreated to the edge of the square, listening to some musicians playing guitar and horns.

Eve met her gaze. "I think you've already met that mysterious stranger." She added softly, "Besides, I'm not just in it for the money. The tips aren't as good as bartending, but it sure as hell beats prostitution. Anyway, I know a few things. My mother was Roma." She ran her fingers over Amber's hand. "You've been lied to and abused." She searched her face. "You've been humiliated."

"How do you know—?"

Eve laughed softly and began turning over her cards. "I don't have to be a seer to know that. It's in how you carry yourself. But I can see something else. You've got steel underneath. You're going to do something—a few things—you may or may not regret." She turned over a card depicting an image of the Grim Reaper. She went white under her makeup. "Someone is going to die."

A shiver worked its way down Amber's spine and penetrated her skin like a pinprick. "Can you see who it will be?" She swallowed. "Or what I'm going to do?"

"I'm not God, but I think you'll know what it is when you have to do it. As to who will die, that is definitely up to God." Eve shrugged and laughed softly. She crossed one arm over the other. "I don't tell people what to do or look into a crystal ball. That's why I'm cheap."

"You don't sound like some of the women who read tarot."

"I know tarot. I know the cards. My mother really is Roma. We're not all failed artists or whores, you know. I have a mission." She laughed softly. "And I'm not an idiot. I was at Loyola, but I made the mistake of sleeping with my professor. He was fired, but I was expelled, too."

Hurley and Amber headed to his car. He held the door for her. Amber was about to slide into her seat when she caught a glimpse of the blond woman from earlier. She almost said something to Hurley, but she sensed he saw the woman as well. He said nothing, only slammed her door and headed to his side of the car. Amber involuntarily shivered. What the hell was going on? Why in hell had she gone to Eve?

The house was on St. Ann Street in the Quarter. It was a typical Creole cottage, square with a tiny brick stoop and small balcony. Tall shutters concealed windows that stretched floor to ceiling. To Amber's surprise, delicate lace curtains graced the square eyes of those windows.

She stood behind Winston as he unlocked the door and stepped aside to let her brush past him. Equally surprising, the living room was filled with ornate, Gothic crosses on the wall and a portrait of a beautiful woman in a blue gown. An antique, porcelain water pitcher occupied a mahogany coffee table. Every piece of furniture was ornate, antique, and priceless.

"Can I interest you in a drink?" Winston indicated a liquor cabinet in the corner.

"We've had lots of wine." Amber swallowed hard. Her heart raced. *Hadn't she had enough of men? Of the shame they brought? Why did she find him so electric?*

Winston made his way to the cabinet and produced two glasses. "That's not an answer. Do you like bourbon?"

Amber nodded. She made her way to him, watching as he produced the bottle and poured them each a glass. "I always remember my dad drinking bourbon."

He handed her a glass and then tipped his to hers. "A man with taste who produced a beautiful daughter." He nodded his approval. His eyes grew misty; he looked away quickly. "And a musician, too. John was lucky."

"I don't think I told you my dad's name." Amber turned to him, startled.

"You did. You just don't remember." The smile never left his scarred face. Or was it a smile? A blackbird screeched outside.

Amber shrugged away her uncertainty and continued, "I haven't felt too beautiful of late." She laughed slightly at the irony. What were they calling her—Porn Queen, Digital Whore? She'd heard that as the kids snickered when she left. Hell, she'd even seen it on a colleague's social networking site. What a bitch! Still, hadn't she brought all of this on herself with her poor judgment, her bad taste in men?

"Why? You did nothing wrong." Winston indicated the grand sofa, lightly took her hand, and led her there.

Amber felt her face grow hot. She sank into the soft cushions of the sofa. "I looked like a whore—at the very least a fool."

Winston shook his head. "No, you're an adult. So was your lover. He was the jerk for abusing your trust." He placed a hand lightly on hers. "I've said it before, and it's true."

Amber suppressed the shiver of delight racing through her being. She'd sworn off the opposite sex. Men had betrayed her. She couldn't afford another stupid mistake. She placed her other hand on his.

Winston lifted her hand to his and kissed it, letting his lips linger there. His gaze met hers. "You are a beautiful woman, Amber. Don't doubt it." He looked down. "I wouldn't expect a woman like you, eh, a young woman, to return—"

Before he finished the words, Amber moved toward him and planted her lips on his. She let her hand roam along Winston's leg and then traced his jeans along the crotch. *Why am I doing this? Why am I so aggressive?* Amber's thoughts raced like a train through her consciousness. *Shouldn't I be done with men?* Her mind said she should while her body responded to this ostensibly unattractive man who filled her senses with desire. She melted into his open embrace, her arms encircling him as he held her in a viselike grip.

Winston's lips caressed hers as his tongue probed the recesses of her mouth. He ran his hands along her blouse and then searched for the buttons, deftly releasing them. He unsnapped her bra with one practiced movement as she released the buckle at his belt and unfastened his zipper. She caressed his cock through his briefs and then reached inside. His member throbbed with her touch. He slid her onto her back, kissing her breasts, her stomach, her thighs, and then the soft flesh between her legs.

Winston caressed her breasts and then pressed her nipples between his fingers. He locked her in his arms, lifted her, and carried her to a back bedroom.

The room was large with a king-sized bed boasting a mahogany bedstead. A small leather sofa occupied the far corner. Mahogany night tables held ornate crystal lamps. A bear rug covered the bed, and, as Winston gently put her across the spread, Amber noticed the mirror above.

Winston knelt down and sucked on her sex, his tongue soothing and arousing her, causing her sweet nectar to flow. He then stood on the side of the bed, pulling her to him and raising her legs to his shoulders. With a single thrust, he plunged his member into her sweet paradise and rocked as she alternately yielded and pushed against him. Then, he crawled over her, straddling her as she wrapped her legs around his waist. He kissed her face, her neck, and then her lips. Amber groaned with pleasure as he sucked on her breasts, luxuriating in his own soft moans of decadent pleasure. It was then he exploded within her, sending his manhood into the depths of her sex.

Later that night, Amber lay beside Winston, sharing bourbon on the rocks. Winston turned on his side and gazed at her, smiling at her exposed breasts.

"You are a lovely meal, young lady, and I'm privileged you wanted me." He paused, took a sip of his drink, and added, "I hope you enjoyed it."

Amber grinned and turned on her side. "Do you doubt it? You were fabulous." She paused and swirled the drink in her hand. "I—I guess I needed that. I needed to see I could trust a man again, and I do trust you."

Winston was silent for a long time, considering something. Amber watched him. The creases in his face grew deeper. Finally, he said, "Do you trust me?"

Amber nodded, frowning. Why was he hesitating?

"Do you like games? Sometimes, they're fun, and nothing happens if you don't want it to."

"What kind of games?" Amber sat up and took a deep sip of her bourbon. The dark liquid flowed soothingly down her throat. The question was moot. She knew what he meant. She'd never tried any games before to know if she was or was not a fan of such things.

"Some people like to dominate. Some like to submit. Some of us like to do both." Winston shrugged. He threw aside the blanket and moved across the room in his nakedness. He was amazingly toned for an older, damaged man, with no softness to his middle, and hard, muscular legs.

The muscles in his arms bulged as he reached for her glass. "Refill?"

Amber nodded. The liquor and the sex filled her senses in a pleasurable way.

He left the room, returning with their glasses filled.

Amber took the glass from him and sat up. She looked at him over her glass. *Why was she so curious, aroused even? Shouldn't the needs of the flesh have evaporated with Tyler's betrayal?* A shiver of anticipation ran through her being as she studied him.

"Bondage?"

Winston lay on his side, swirling the liquid in his glass. "Some. Only if you like it." He paused, caressing her hand. "Sometimes punishing others—or ourselves—can cleanse the soul." He gave her that appealingly crooked smile. "It can give us a sense of redemption."

Amber looked into his eyes. What secrets did he hold? She sensed great hurt and loss somewhere in his being. Whom had he hurt that he needed redemption?

"Do you think I need redemption?" Her voice was no more than a whisper. She didn't see any condemnation in his face, but others would condemn her. She didn't want to lie in shame.

"You're perfect, darling. Did you ever consider I might need to be redeemed? I wore the uniform for Uncle Sam. All of us need to be redeemed." He stood and reached for his shirt. "Think about it. Only when you're ready. Tonight, we can go hear some music at Kerry's." He buttoned the shirt and winked at her.

# Chapter Five

## Early December 2017

Amber thought about little else besides Winston's proposition until she finally decided to agree.

What haunted Amber the most was why she had even considered the proposal. She'd been through enough with men, hadn't she? Why was she so willing to expose herself to another potential hurt or scandal?

Amber found herself preparing for his return in ways she never had with Tyler. She visited the beauty salon where they tinted her hair with shades of blue and then submitted to another hour of grooming while a woman painted her nails so that they simulated a star pattern. Deciding her skirts were too long, she visited shops on Magazine Street, selecting dresses and skirts in exotic patterns or deep colors.

Winston returned after a week. Amber heard his key in the door, rose from the sofa on which she'd been reading, and walked the long hallway to meet him. He placed his lone bag on the floor and smiled at her crookedly, the guitar case slung over his shoulder.

Amber shivered slightly, not knowing why. It wasn't fear. Anticipation, maybe? She knew that whatever he wanted, she wouldn't deny it to him.

"Can I get you something? How was your trip? Do you want anything?"

The words came in a rush. Winston's grin grew broader. He gingerly placed the guitar in the corner and said, "Only you."

The words sent a sliver of thrill through her whole being. Amber took his hand, led him to the kitchen, and poured Jameson and ginger for both of them into the delicate crystal cups in the cupboard. "I hope I put enough ice."

"It's fine." He winked at her. "I have something for you in my bag. I hope you like it."

"I will." Amber winced inwardly. Why did she agree with him so easily? He never abused her or demanded anything, but his personality was dominant. She succumbed—maybe too easily.

"Meet me in the bedroom." Winston handed her his drink and walked out of the room without another word.

Amber made her way down the hall, pushed open the bedroom door, and sat on the bed which she'd covered with a leopard print spread. Her heart beat rapidly as his shadow grew in the hallway. Even his shadowy image filled her with excitement and trepidation. She downed her drink with one quick gulp. She heard him talking softly to Alwena, offering her a treat and placing them in her bowl in the kitchen.

Winston entered the bedroom, deposited his bag on the floor and held out a wrapped package to Amber. "You'll look gorgeous in this."

Amber took the box from him. It was adorned in red paper and a bow so purple it looked black. She sat on the bed and carefully unwrapped it. The tissue gave way, only to reveal a black corset, black lace stockings with pirate insignia, and a black lace garter belt. A petite, deep blue nightie lay nestled at the very bottom.

She took the garter belt in her hand and fingered the intricate lace. "What will you wear?" The words were out of her mouth before she knew she'd voiced them. She felt her face grow hot.

"Don't worry. Sometimes, I'll dominate, too. This is all for pleasure"— he paused and took a sip of his drink—"and a way of atoning for sins."

"Do you think I'm a sinner?" Amber dropped the belt back into the box. Her heart was racing as blood pulsed through her veins.

"We're all sinners, darling. Didn't I tell you my father was a preacher?" Winston placed his drink on a night table and moved closer to her. "We all have the stain of original sin."

"I—I'm not sure I can dominate." Amber swallowed hard.

"When you're ready. Only then. You're not being forced into anything. Things can stop whenever you want them to." He gave her that crooked smile. "Do you trust me to blindfold you?"

A sensation seared through Amber—one she couldn't identify. Why was this man so appealing? How was he twisting her to his will? Well, he wasn't twisting her. That polite Texas drawl accompanied every suggestion, every request, and every touch.

When he made his way down the hall, Amber donned the blue nightie—just her size—and lay across the bed. She'd never done anything even vaguely like sado-masochism. The idea was foreign to her, yet here she was, waiting for a man old enough to be her father to abuse her. Why was she titillated? Her breasts stood hard and erect as she lightly fingered them through the most delicate of lace.

Upon his return, Winston wore what Amber recognized as a jockey's accouterments, however, his pants were tight leather. His member bulged inside the skin of whatever animal had died to make his attire. He gripped a riding whip in his hand and tipped it to his jockey's cap.

"You are an image there, Sweet Blossom ." He grinned at her, that strangely appealing crooked grin. "Are you ready to be ridden by a prizewinning jockey?"

A mixture of fear and desire swept over Amber. Her body had a mind of its own. Almost without her knowing what she was doing, she swept the delicate lace from her breasts, exposing them in their pert sensitivity. Her blood pulsed within her veins. What would he do to her in this remote section of the Quarter? Who would hear her cries except drunks and homeless men eager for their own sexual delights? Still, desire rippled through her fear. She smiled at him, a soft laugh escaping her lips almost against her will. She felt her lips curve into a sensual, conspiratorial smile.

Winston reached into the night table and removed a black velvet cloth with one adept motion. Looming over her, he tied it around her eyes. She rose slightly from the bed as he did so, but then he forcefully pushed her down. She gasped, startled but unhurt and caught between a combination of trepidation and aching need.

Amber's insides turned to a deep liquid as his fingers stroked her soft skin. Every sense in her body vibrated with a deep resonance as he slightly pinched her nipples and then wrapped his lips around them. She felt her sex grow wet and as hot as a volcano.

Winston slipped the thong from her legs, revealing her sex. She heard him sigh. Was he luxuriating in her scent, she wondered, memorizing the scent of her sex? She then felt him clasp her hands in a viselike grip. She winced. He released one but clasped the other. She heard the nightstand drawer opening again and felt the cold hardness of metal against her skin as he extended first one arm and then the other behind her, twisting her body so that her head was now on the pillow. So he'd handcuffed her to the bed but cared enough about her comfort to see that her head was comfortable. Amber almost laughed. So far, he'd done nothing that a hero in an erotic novel wouldn't do. Was this a modern adaptation of a pornographic, modern, chivalric King Arthur? Did he and Guinevere share these erotic moments?

Then, Winston was between her legs. She could feel him as he parted her thighs and grew intimately close to her. His hand lightly caressed her most intimate parts. Then, his fingers explored the folds of her sex, touching her deepest parts—her slit, her quim—arousing her so that she gasped to suppress the scream of delight that threatened. A shiver of excitement raced down her spine, making her quiver with delight. That she was helpless, at his mercy, sent her heart pounding with excitement, pleasure, and a fear that was erotic. She felt the bumps on her skin come alive. Then, he moved his tongue along her legs, along her mound and finally into her sex. He lingered there, savoring her. She couldn't see him but sensed he was before her, on his knees, bent over her private parts. It was then she felt his pulsing member against her thighs, wet and as hot as lava. Suddenly, swiftly, he turned her over.

"Do you want me to continue?" Winston's voice held the heat of a Texas summer.

"Yes, my lord." The archaic address came instinctively. The handcuffs cut into her wrists. She bit her lip, willing herself not to call out. She would show him she wasn't weak. She, the sacrifice, was a match for him and anything he could inflict.

The crop came down swift and hard against her buttocks. Seven hard strokes. Amber bit her lips and suppressed the cries that rose within her throat. Then, he stopped and turned her onto her back. She felt the device against her thighs and then the cheek of her vagina.

Winston first stroked her himself. He touched the bud of her womanhood and then deeply inside her sex, sighing as he did so. Then, the vibrator. Expertly, gently, and then with force, he moved it along her crevices until she felt her insides burn even hotter and harder. He thrust her legs upward. She felt her feet against his shoulders. She drew in a breath as he loomed over her and lifted her buttocks slightly up.

"Are you ready, Sweet Blossom?"

"Yes, my lord."

His member was thick and hard upon penetration. Amber didn't suppress the cries of wild abandon she experienced as her wrists strained against the cuffs. He filled her completely, stroking her throbbing breasts and the softness of her stomach as he choked on his own cries of pleasure. Then, he collapsed against her, breathing like a swimmer too long underwater.

Later, Amber leaned against Winston as they shared wine and cheese together in bed. He'd treated her wrists with salve and bound them with light gauze. Amber munched on the tray of exotic cheeses and fruit he'd gathered from the kitchen.

Why did she feel so alive yet so shaken? Her behavior in his arms had violated every moral with which she'd been reared, yet Amber had luxuriated at the thrill of the man's touch. His abuse had left her craving more, and Amber winced at her response to such treatment. Well, who was she to judge? Her love affair with Tyler hadn't been tame or proper. She'd thought it was private and still hated her former lover for his betrayal; however, Amber knew that what she'd done with Tyler himself had been indiscreet at the very least. Still, she was happy to lie in her new lover's arms.

Alwena had propelled herself onto the bed and received the pieces of bread Amber gifted her with the air of a queen accepting gifts from her subjects.

"I hope you didn't mind my asking about your visit with your son. I was just curious about where you went." She paused, took a bite of her cheese, and said, "I missed you."

"Well, I'm glad to hear you missed me, darling." Winston stroked her still-throbbing wrists. He sighed heavily. "It's always hard when I see Julian. We're not estranged, but my boy hasn't been the same since his mother died. It was hard for him. He's grown now—" Winston's voice caught. "That's all I have to say."

Amber leaned against him and encircled him in her arms. "I'm sorry you're hurting. I'm sorry your son is."

"It's been years, but her death was a terrible thing, a horrible—"

He stopped suddenly, his mouth set in a firm line. His voice took on a hard edge. Amber sensed he wanted to open up but couldn't—or wouldn't.

"I'm sorry. I never speak of her."

For the rest of the night, they lay together in bed, watching movies as they stroked each other tenderly. Alwena curled into a ball and fell asleep.

# Chapter Six

"Can we meet for coffee?"

Amber heard the voice over the phone, incredulous. "Why would I want to have coffee with you as if you were a friend, Adrienne? You betrayed me. You and Tyler laughed at me."

"I—I didn't mean to hurt you, Amber. I swear that. What happened with Tyler just happened. We didn't plan it. At least I didn't—" Adrienne's voice rose to a shrill shriek.

"What in hell do you mean? You're not a kid, Adrienne, even though you've been pampered your whole life." Amber felt the blood pulsing inside her veins. Why was she wasting time with a selfish brat?

She was alone in the house except for Alwena. She sat down heavily at the kitchen table, a mug of coffee in the other hand. Winston was on the road yet again. Amber liked the peace of the house. Why was the little brat interrupting her first cup of coffee?

"Yeah, that's what you and all of those people at the school think of me. Well, I wasn't born with a silver spoon. I've had to work."

"Your father owns a fast food franchise. You don't know what work is. You've taught less than two years."

Amber stared at her cell phone, her hand poised to hit the button to end the call. Hypocritical, sniveling people really disgusted her, and Adrienne reminded her of her humiliation at the hands of her ex-boyfriend and her employers. She wished Adrienne would find a deep hole, lose her balance and fall in. Amber fantasized about attending her funeral in a red dress.

Adrienne spoke rapidly. "Look, there's something you need to know about Tyler. That's why I wanted to talk to you, but I won't say it over the phone."

"Okay, I'm listening." Amber hated to admit she was intrigued. What in hell did the little bitch mean?

"Not over the phone. Meet me at Café Du Monde for coffee at ten. We can talk there." With that, the phone went dead.

Amber arrived at Café Du Monde promptly at the agreed-upon time, went to the counter, ordered her coffee and made her way to a table. Tourists and locals mingled over steaming café au lait and hot beignets. She took in the assorted people.

The tourists were easy to spot. They walked around in Hawaiian shirts and shorts, cameras hanging from their necks. The locals were often accompanying them, showing out-of-town guests the uniqueness of the city.

Amber noticed Adrienne as she made her way to the line for coffee. She made eye contact with Amber and quickly strode over to the table. Why in hell did she always dress in a skirt and heels even for the most casual of meetings? Was she so vain?

"Thanks for meeting me." Adrienne took a sip of her coffee. She looked around uneasily. "Have you found a job? It's mid-year. Some people hire in December."

"No, I haven't. I have"—Amber hesitated momentarily and then added—"other business opportunities."

"Well, good for you. My dad's offered me a job, but I don't know. I liked teaching. The pay was lousy, but you have all the holidays." Adrienne shrugged and looked away. She was wearing glasses and pushed them up the bridge of her nose.

Weariness suddenly invaded Amber's bones. She sighed heavily and tried to keep the edge out of her voice. She wanted this little conference over.

"Look, Adrienne, it's not as if we're friends just meeting for coffee anymore. You stabbed me in the back." She took a sip of coffee; the warm liquid soothed her throat.

"It was Tyler. He—"

"Save it. Maybe he was the seducer, but you weren't raped. You thought he loved you, and hey, had it been love and you two would have come clean, I'd have accepted it. I may have been hurt, but I would have understood that you can't deny certain feelings. But no, you two sneaked around like criminals." She swallowed hard but pushed back the hurt that threatened to engulf her whole being. No, she wouldn't show how much Adrienne's betrayal had hurt. "You're just—"

Adrienne held up a hand. Her lower lip trembled, and her voice cracked. "Please, stop. You don't understand. I found out something about Tyler."

"What? That he didn't love you either. He made that clear." Amber's voice was a hiss.

"No, you don't understand. He's related to Trish." Adrienne leaned in closer. "I think that bitch set us up with Tyler. He's a cousin. He set us up for a fall."

"Come on, Adrienne. You can't be serious." Amber thought of Trish as a devious bitch, but that she would launch a whole conspiracy seemed absurd. How delusional was this girl sitting across from her?

"No, I'm not making this up." Adrienne shook her head frantically. "Her dad was military, but their roots are here. You know how she lived with a grandmother for a while? Well, Tyler's one of her cousins."

Amber shook her head. She clutched the cup so tightly her knuckles turned white. "How do you know this? She lived all over the country and world. As you said, her dad was military." Amber considered it, thinking aloud. "Look, my mother had some negative history with her, but you didn't. Why would she hurt you?"

Adrienne ignored her comment and forged on. "I went to a wedding a few days ago. I was talking to a guy who turned out to be one of Tyler's high school friends. He knew Trish, too. He hinted there was a reason she had to move here with her grandmother. He said she'd done some pretty nasty stuff."

"Like what?" Amber's anger had vanished; an unsettling curiosity crept into her consciousness.

"He didn't say."

"Okay, you're making this up." Amber took one last gulp of her coffee and made as if to stand.

"This friend only knew her once she moved here, but he heard she'd caused problems for her parents in Texas during one of their posts. They sent her to her grandmother." Adrienne placed a hand on Amber's arm. "You have relatives there, too, don't you? Military, in fact."

"My dad's cousin, yes." Amber gazed hard at Adrienne. "What are you saying? Trish set us up? Okay, she didn't like my family, but why would she set you up? She had nothing against you."

"She gave my job to a friend of hers." Adrienne sighed deeply. She twisted her hands together on the table, looking around as if she expected eavesdroppers to emerge from the woodwork. "I haven't found anything yet. She had plans for our jobs. I heard another friend of hers is the new librarian."

Amber shrugged. "I have a business arrangement."

"Maybe you could find out about what happened in Texas from your cousin. Someone must know something about this woman. It's like she just appeared."

"No, not the case. Her mother was from here and hated my mother. She resented my mother's stability. It's no secret her family's screwed up. Besides, Texas is a big state. I don't know that my cousin knew her parents. What do you expect me to find?" Amber wiped her hands with the napkin and stood. *As if I'd share what I knew with you anyway.*

"You could get something on her. She sits in her position too damned secure. You know that. The archdiocese thinks she walks on water. Why not bring her down a peg?" Adrienne almost hissed the words. "Your cousin is military. Chances are he knew her family in some way."

"It's the past. I'm over it. You should get over it, too." Even as Amber spoke, she knew her words were untrue. If it were possible, she would get even with the bitch Trish.

Amber winced inside. How much had she denied her whole life? She could taste the possible revenge but had never thought herself a hateful person. For that matter, how much had she denied about her own desire and sexual nature? All her life she'd been the "good little girl"; the boys she'd dated as a teen had thought her "too respectable" because she hadn't "put out." Even the young men in college had resented her discriminate taste, even after she'd long lost her virginity. Well, too bad. Winston Hurley had awakened something in her—something primal, disturbing, and exciting.

*** 

"Are you ready to punish me?" Winston looked at Amber over a glass of red wine as they ate at Muriel's in Jackson Square.

The words caught Amber by surprise. She was about to take a bite of fish, her fork paused in midair. "I—I don't know. I've never done it before."

"You'd never been punished before, either, but you adapted, didn't you?" He smiled at her. His voice was soft, gentlemanly, so very Texan.

Amber swallowed hard. Her heart pounded. For a few minutes, the silence was so thick she could hear the clink of other diners' glasses.

"Why do you need punishment? You don't seem to be some great sinner."

"Remember, I told you my daddy was a preacher. He was a real hypocrite, but he did teach me about sin and that forbidden fruit." He poured wine into her glass.

"You said you didn't get along with him. Why let him guilt trip you?" Amber felt her whole body grow warm. Was it embarrassment or a strange titillation? She felt her lips curve into that involuntary, sensual smile.

"We all feel guilt, darling, even when we hate the source of it." He observed her with that same intense gaze and oh-so-gentlemanly Texas drawl.

"Maybe so." Amber thought of her own times with Tyler and the way she'd enjoyed their erotic play. Why were people so abandoned when they think the curtains are drawn? If their secret desires remain secret, they live with the façade of respectability. It's when someone thrusts the curtains aside that their warts are revealed to the glaring light. It's only then they blush.

She swallowed her savory food, her whole being growing warm. "I—I'll do what you ask."

Winston nodded. "There's a room you haven't seen."

Amber knew that room. She'd tried the knob. It was across from the bedroom. When she'd mentioned it to him, Winston had told her never to open it. His tone had been so intense she'd shivered, but then, he'd winked at her and feigned a lightness she didn't believe. *What dark secrets did he have? Why was she becoming such a willing participant in his secret games?*

Amber walked back to the house with Winston, clutching his hand. She glanced at him in the moonlight. His lips were set in a thin line, and the scars marring what once may have been a handsome face seemed even deeper, more intense.

Winston turned to her as he inserted the key to open the door. "Nothing will happen you don't want, but it's your turn to punish me."

"I can't imagine you needing punishing." Amber looked hard at him. "You're always so gentlemanly."

Pushing the door open, he said as he stepped in, "We all have a past."

Amber followed him inside as he switched on the lights. She clasped her midsection and swallowed, feeling suddenly cold. "I get that all too well. The past can come back to haunt us."

She bent to scratch Alwena's ears. The dog gave her what appeared to be a quizzical look. She bent back her ears and then marched down the hall with her tail up.

"True, but yours is a more recent past. Some of us have long shadows."

Amber suddenly realized they'd traversed the hall and now stood in front of the room at the back of the shotgun. Alwena stood beside her, glanced quickly at Amber, whimpered and then turned in the direction of the kitchen. She cast a look at Amber before entering the kitchen.

Winston extracted a key from his jacket pocket and inserted it into the lock. Amber noted that it was an ordinary lock, no deadbolt or high tech device. What was he guarding so determinedly? Well, she soon would find out.

Winston swung open the door and switched on the light. The room sprung to life with a luminous glow. Amber involuntarily gasped as horror swept over her whole being. A cage occupied most of the floor. It was large enough to house a jungle cat or other wild animal. Whips hung from the wall from massive hooks. Handcuffs hung on smaller hooks below the whips. A wicker basket occupied a corner of the room, but what drew Amber's eye was the massive wooden cross erected against the center of the wall. It had been nailed into the wall; the wood was unfinished and coarse.

She turned to him. "Wh—what is all this?"

"Well, remember I said my daddy was a preacher. Jesus suffered torture for our sins. If you want punishment, you should follow his example." Winston removed his broad cowboy hat and tossed it on the ornately carved chair in the corner.

Amber swallowed and turned slowly in the direction of the cage. "What is that?"

He grinned. "A cage."

Anger stirred in Amber's breast. She said sharply, "I know that. Why is it here?"

Winston moved to her, taking her face in his hands. His fingers caressed her cheeks and then stroked her head. "Imagine the plight of a wild jungle cat. He must feel terrible trapped like that. God knows what kind of punishment that feels like." His hands caressed her face tenderly. "Imagine wanting mercy from your captor. You'd loved to be free, but you can't be. That's how the poor animal must feel. Sometimes, humans must feel the same way. Imagine it. You want release from pain and forgiveness, but you don't know what to do."

Amber studied him, and her heart contracted with pity. The man was suffering, and she wanted to end that pain. How had she grown so attached to him? To everything about him? He was shrouded in mystery, a true enigma, but that made him all the more appealing. She'd loved what she thought was Tyler's openness, but he'd been nothing but a lying scumbag. Winston made it clear there were things he didn't want to say, but that was okay with Amber. She'd rather a man who was honest about having a dark past than a man who lied about his present.

She swallowed hard. Instinctively, Amber knew she'd do whatever he wanted. "What will help? How can I help?"

"Don't look so sad, little darling. I'm a big boy, and I can deal with my pain. Still, having a beauty like you alleviate it always refreshes the soul." He shot that crooked smile in her direction.

Amber's heart pounded with the stirrings of desire. She clenched his hand that had cradled her face and raised it to her lips. She gently let her lips linger and then subtly bit the palm of his hand. Lightly, she stroked his cock.

Winston drew in a breath, closed his eyes with a deep sigh, and then rubbed his hand. A tiny drop of blood had developed on his palm. He indicated a standing closet. "You'll find what you need in there."

Amber made her way to the old-fashioned, wooden closet and turned the antique key. Her maternal grandmother had had one very like it. Inside was the ebony corset, the pirate stockings of black lace, the metal handcuffs. Hanging from a hook in the back was a long whip. Gathering up the items, she asked over her shoulder, "May I go into the facilities? Have some privacy to change?"

Winston gave her a sweeping bow. "Of course. A gentleman always allows a lady her privacy."

Amber felt her cheeks grow hot. Casting a glance at the whip, she clutched the corset and stockings to her, looked at him, and then padded down the hall.

She ducked into the bedroom, quickly cast off her clothes, and slipped into the stockings. A garter belt was attached to one of them. The silky material glided over her flesh, sending a surge of energy and shimmering anticipation down her spine. She carefully hooked the buttons on the garter and then slid the corset over her body.

Running her tongue over her lips, Amber adjusted the hooks across her breasts and midsection. The lace along the corset wasn't new. Amber saw the telltale signs of worn material. Whoever had worn it before was her size. *Did Winston simply find women of the same body build and appearance? What about the same personality? Had he noticed her perched atop that barstool in Texas and seen a woman ripe for plucking?* Amber had never seen herself as beautiful, yet this damaged man found her a delectable fantasy. Of course, her parents had called her beautiful. So had Tyler. But all parents saw their children as beautiful. And Tyler, well, she knew all too well how good his word was.

Amber made her way back to the secret room. Winston stood before her, the whip in his hand. He held it out to her. When she didn't take it, he thrust it aside. It made a hissing sound as it hit the ground. "The cross or the cage?"

Amber's stomach churned. She swallowed hard. "I—I don't think I'm ready for the cross yet. I'm too good a Catholic school girl."

Winston grinned lopsidedly at her. "I can understand that. We Baptists have lots of guilt." He paused as if hesitating. "You'll strip me, right?"

Amber found herself smiling—as if her body reacted to this man against her will. She moved close to him and began unbuttoning his silk shirt, feeling his breath against her face, feathering her stray strands of hair. *Where did he get his money? Who was this man supporting her in grand style even when he disappeared?* A sliver of fear accompanied by a wave of excitement raced through her whole being.

As he fumbled unsuccessfully with his shirt, she moved to his pants, her fingers working clumsily along his belt and then his zipper. The longhorn, the University of Texas insignia, shone along the belt buckle. She knew nothing of his past, and in many ways, that made this tryst with him all the more exciting. Tyler had been an open book—or so he'd let on. A white-bread boy from the burbs who'd wooed her with sweet words, yet his intentions had been dark from the start, she suspected. Well, this Texan had that oh-so-gentlemanly twang, but he made no pretense of being some rube with no past. No, he was a grown man and experienced. She liked that, and she liked seeing his bulging member as she stroked him through the tight-fitting denim.

He was fit for a man she suspected was over sixty. *What had happened to him to so mar his face? Then, there were the scars she'd seen along his back.*

. . Well, he wanted to be punished, but she would only move on his direction. She unfastened his zipper, pushed down his pants and then the tight underwear. A ripple of lust spread from her belly to her chest. She began gingerly unbuttoning the shirt that bound him. Then, he ripped it off, tearing the buttons away.

Amber laughed, licked his taut chest, and pinched his small nipples until he called out in a mixture of pain and pleasure. Gently, she knelt and took him in her mouth and listened to his groans. Releasing him, she gazed up at him, reveling in his pleasure. He smiled down at her, stroked her cheek, and raised her. He cast an appreciative look her way—taking in the contours of her body in the costume.

"Don't forget the whip." Winston cast a glance at her over his shoulder as he strode to the cage naked. It was large enough to hold a man or any wild animal—two animals for that matter. He knelt and then went onto all fours. "You'll get in later. For right now, you'll discipline me."

"Through the cage?" Amber's voice was a whisper and sounded hollow in her own ears. She collected the whip from the floor. It felt coarse in her hands, but she had to play the part. She had to perform as he wanted. Wordlessly, she cracked it. This was no crop. This was a bullwhip.

"Yes, just follow my lead." With that, he crawled into the cage. "Crack the whip."

"I'll hurt you."

"I know, darling. Do it, Mistress." His voice changed with the last sentence. He was more pleading, hurting.

Amber nodded slowly. Hesitantly, she cracked the whip. He cried out, winced, and held his midsection.

"Harder, Mistress! Make me hurt!" His voice was harsh, cold, demanding!

"Do you really want to suffer?" Amber sensed her voice wasn't harsh enough, demanding enough. That's what he'd wanted. He wanted to suffer. The scene repelled and excited her at the same time.

"Yes, I told you so. Take the lead." He gazed at her through the bars of the cage. "You must do this, Mistress."

Amber nodded and let the whip fly. It penetrated the cracks in the cage and tore Winston's flesh as he leaned against the cold metal, his gaze following her every movement.

He cried out but wet his lips. "Come in now. You know you want to, Mistress."

Amber steeled herself as she threw open the door to his prison. She stood before him in her corset gripping the whip tightly in both hands. "What do you want me to do?"

"Punish me as you see fit. You have to lead." He took a cloth suspended from a bar of the cage. "Blindfold me, Mistress."

Amber mechanically moved toward him. Taking the black cloth from him, she secured it around his eyes. Her own hands felt moist. Perspiration dotted her face. She felt wet under the corset.

Winston stood passively before her. Suddenly, he began speaking in a way she could only describe as hypnotic. "I'm everyone you've ever hated—that boyfriend who betrayed you. The friend you hate just as much." He paused a long time, letting the words sink into her psyche. "The administration that was so unjust to you."

Amber blinked back tears. The anger and sense of betrayal returned. She cracked the whip wide. She wanted him to stop, to shut his fucking mouth. Then, she lashed out in his direction.

Winston cried out, doubled over, and then began laughing in a way she could only describe as maniacal. "That's it, Mistress. Let me have it." Blood oozed from a gash on his arm. He momentarily clutched the wound and then let his hand fall; blood dotted the cage.

Amber let the whip fly again. This time it landed on his midsection, not drawing blood but leaving a welt. "Oh, Jesus," she murmured. "Give me strength."

Again he cried out and then laughed. Tears rolled down his cheeks. "Come to me. Leave the whip, Mistress. Hurt me more personal."

Amber gasped. She'd never hurt anyone like that before. She shook from head to toe when she dropped the whip and ran for him, hands flailing. Struggling against his powerful arms, she bit at his neck and his chest while he laughed hysterically. His arms relaxing, he let her get near so that her teeth scratched his flesh. The blood from his arm now dotted her face. She pounded his chest until he caught her arms and bellowed, "Enough!"

Winston was suddenly kissing her violently, his lips boring into her own as he pushed her mouth open with his tongue. He thrust her on the floor and then loomed over her. Turning onto his back, he said gently, "Ride me, Mistress, ride me. Take off that restrictive thing—please."

Amber noted his swing from aggressor back to submissive. *Why was this so titillating?* Her nipples were tight and pert in the corset as she slipped it off and then rolled onto him. She mounted him and slid onto his erect member, moving her pelvis to the gyrations of his own hips. Stroking his balls, she let the feeling of exultation wash over her as he reached up to stroke her tingling breasts.

"Hit me!" His voice held a command.

Mechanically at first and then with passion, she began striking his thighs with the hand not stroking his balls. Her own pleasure mounted as he groaned with abandon under her, mumbling, "I love your pussy. Do you love my cock inside you?" Then, his cock erupted inside Amber as she felt the stirrings of molten passion seethe through her body. Exhausted, she collapsed beside him.

# Chapter Seven

Three weeks before Christmas

Amber sat in Kerry's Irish Pub, sipping one of their famous Irish coffees. It was late afternoon, and Winston had embarked on what he termed a "business" trip. Her laptop open before her, she stared at her vita while reveling in the mixture of whipped cream, caffeine, and whiskey. *Health food*, she thought with that familiar Catholic schoolgirl feeling of guilt and delight.

Well, she couldn't live on Winston forever. She'd put off her mother's questions about her apartment. Vanessa had asked when she could stop by for coffee; Amber had put her off and dropped into her mother's home instead. What would Vanessa say if she knew of this bizarre arrangement? Amber blushed to consider what her mother would think; no, she would pretend to be in her own apartment for as long as she could. Then, Amber didn't know how long this arrangement would last. She had to find a job and look out for her own future. She was a librarian with a master's degree and numerous credentials to her credit.

As she perfected minor details, Amber became aware of someone watching her from Decatur Street, the same woman who had snapped photos of her with Winston. She buried herself in her project, attempting to ignore the woman who was staring so pointedly at her. Even though she'd only seen her from a distance, Amber was sure it was the same woman. *What in hell did she want?* Amber's behavior had been indiscreet, but her videos hadn't gone so viral that any journalist or writer from some rag would be interested in her. Winston might be strangely disfigured, but he sure wasn't so fascinating that some writer, photographer, or morbidly curious person would seek him out.

Amber made corrections to the vita and began the cover letter. When she looked up, the woman had crossed the street and was making her way into the pub. She walked to the bar, ordered a Guinness, and crossed to stand beside Amber's table.

"May I join you?" Her voice was crisp. Amber detected a Boston accent. She held out a hand when Amber hesitated. "I'm Mary Stone. I freelance for several rock journals. I'd like to talk to you."

Amber recognized the name. The woman had been an award-winning writer in her younger days before various addictions and a slanderous piece on a young rock star ruined her reputation. Reputable journals wouldn't touch her, and she had decided to write salacious and tawdry novels. The books had sold, and some journals were willing to work with her on a freelance level. However, these were not the most honorable or reputable of magazines.

Amber turned her attention to her computer. "How may I help you, Ms. Stone? I'm very busy."

"How much do you know about the man you're now living with? How much has he told you about his past?" The woman took a notebook from a small briefcase. The camera was still hanging from her neck.

"As I said, I'm very busy, and I don't see how any of this is your business." Amber pointedly glanced around the pub. "There are lots of tables here. Why don't you find one? I'm too preoccupied for conversation."

"You should know what you're getting into. I hate to see a young woman involved in something sordid or possibly illegal." Mary scribbled in her notebook.

"I'm a house sitter, and I don't see how any of this concerns you or what possible interest it could be to a magazine. Let me alone or I'll tell the bartender. He's a friend and will get rid of you."

Mary ran a hand along the strap of her camera. "Okay, but listen to this. Have you asked him about how his wife died? About that son of his? How he learned to play guitar like this? About the Gulf War and what he did? Do you know the implications of being involved in fraud and even murder?"

The words sent a shiver down Amber's spine, but she kept her features neutral. Her voice was a hiss. "Everyone has a past. Some people's pasts are sadder than others, and I want you to—"

"Yes, I've heard about your little, er, escapades." Mary grinned.

Amber stared coldly at her. Anger gripped her like a vise. "I don't know what you mean."

"I think you do, but I'm not interested in you. Your affairs are none of my concern, but if Hurley is who I think he is, those morons who have dissed me will beg for me to write again." Mary slid the notebook into her briefcase.

"I'm not listening to your trash. Stay away from me." Amber turned to call the tall, bald bartender, but Mary quickly stood, gathered her things, and sprinted into the street. Amber stared until she was out of sight, but Mary Stone was right about one thing. There was much Amber didn't know about the man named Winston Hurley.

"I've started sending my resumes out," Amber called to Winston as she poured coffee for herself and him that Saturday morning at the kitchen counter. She came to sit beside him in the living room.

A bluebird chirped outside the window. The air had turned briskly cold and windy. Winston had kindled the fireplace in the living room. The fire alternately roared and gasped as she curled up beside him on the sofa.

"What don't you like about house-sitting for me?" Winston sipped his coffee and looked over the cup at her.

"I—I love it, but I need to support myself and find a job. I'm a certified librarian. Before that, I was a history teacher. I'm better in the library, and sponging off you isn't something I'm totally comfortable with." She studied him and felt herself blush. She didn't always like admitting—even within the depths of her own soul—how much she enjoyed the experimental aspect of their relationship. "You've been great to me, but I was brought up to make my own way in the world." She tucked her feet under her butt and snuggled close to him.

"I see. An independent young woman. That's good. I admire people with work ethic, but remember, there's no rush." He hesitated. "You're not getting tired of other aspects of our arrangement, are you?"

Amber took a deep sip of the strong liquid and let it slide down her throat. She enjoyed the arrangement more than she wanted to admit. She liked living in such a nice place, and the sex at times repelled her but at other times thrilled her. This wasn't something she wanted to leave. "No, I wouldn't want to leave you, but I need a real job."

Winston grinned at her. "That stubborn work ethic. Okay, I get it."

"Besides," Amber kept her voice neutral, not wanting to sound overtly curious. "You can't keep supporting me. It's not fair to you. This place must cost a fortune."

Winston gave her that lopsided smile. "I don't have to worry about money. There's more than enough." He added with that Texas drawl, all charm. "I'm a senior citizen, ma'am, I have a pension."

Amber returned his smile. "All the more reason why I should find a job. I can't take advantage of a senior citizen on a fixed income."

"Well, I'm not quite decrepit, you know. I'd think you'd have figured that one out by now." He laughed outright. "I'd tell you if I couldn't afford to keep you here, but it's no problem."

Amber tried to sound casual. "I just hope I'm not keeping you from other people who might need you or seek you out. You mentioned a son."

"You're not. As for my son, well, we see each other from time to time, but he's deployed a lot."

"Military? Wow, didn't you mention serving in the Gulf? It's admirable that your son—"

"Yeah, it is." He frowned, the scars forming a deep scowl. "I don't think I mentioned the Gulf. I said I wore the uniform, but I didn't say where."

Amber immediately recognized her blunder. Some Mary Stone gossip. "I—I'm sure you did." She swallowed and added, "After all, how would I know?" Well, maybe she'd have to be careful about what she remembered from the Mary Stone conversation. She was curious but wouldn't push it.

Winston stared at her briefly but grinned. "Yeah, how would you? Anyway, aside from Julian, there really isn't any family to speak of." He patted her leg. "Hey, those were some good pancakes you made. Any left?"

Amber nodded with a smile. She recognized it as a dismissal and made her way down the hall to the kitchen. Had she revealed too much? She was certain he'd revealed much more than he wanted to. She also knew Mary Stone knew or suspected more than she was saying.

***

"Honey, is everything okay?"

Amber looked at Vanessa and sighed. Her mother could always read her. She shrugged.

"Sure, why do you ask?"

They were preparing dinner in her mother's comfortable Canal Boulevard kitchen. The house was in a family-oriented, tree-lined section of New Orleans marked by churches and cemeteries.

"Okay, let's not play." Vanessa stirred the meat sauce and then faced Amber, her hands on her hips.

"What do you mean?" Amber emptied the bag of spaghetti into the boiling pot of water. She avoided Vanessa's stare.

Alwena gave her what appeared to be a quizzical look. If the dog had eyebrows, she would have raised one. She then glanced in Vanessa's direction and curled up in the corner. Why did her look say, "You're going to get it now"?

"Like I said, don't play. I've asked you if you need anything, any money. I've also asked you if you want to come home. You don't have a job yet, and you're not living in your apartment."

Amber's heart began to pound furiously in her breast. "Who told you that?" Amber wanted to kill that person, whomever it was.

"Jen. I saw her at the grocery. She said she went to the apartment to check on you. Someone else was living there. She didn't know what to think. Then, she said she called you on your cell, and you were evasive. You put her off about meeting for lunch."

Amber drew in an exasperated breath. Jen Brocato had been her friend since grade school, but Amber had told no one about the depths to which she'd committed herself to Winston Hurley—not her mother and not her friends. Jen especially was in a very stable relationship with a handsome fiancé. She wouldn't even begin to understand how a woman could engage in such behavior.

Amber only said, "I'm house-sitting, Mama. I told you that. I live there for now." Well, she hadn't told Vanessa everything.

"You didn't tell me you'd given up your apartment." Vanessa turned to her cooking. "Does this man you're working for pay you enough?"

"Yes, but I am looking for another job as a librarian. That's my training." Amber stirred the spaghetti, purposefully not meeting her mother's gaze.

"Is that all there is?" Vanessa stared at her as she filled a glass with water from the tap and then poured it into the coffeepot.

Amber frowned, saying innocently, "Mama, what do you mean?"

"Is this mystery man more to you than an employer?" Vanessa placed a spoon into the pot and sampled her sauce. She gave Amber a sideways glance.

"No, of course not. He's much older and just travels a lot." Amber hoped she sounded sincere. She'd told no one that her benefactor was the talented guitarist from Austin. She also wouldn't tell her mother just what her services included.

"I see." Vanessa didn't sound convinced. She added quickly, "Okay, if you are looking for another job, I may have a lead for you. I saw Nicole Smith today. She's the secretary for the principal at Lakeview High, that private school. She and I belong to the same book club. You remember Landon Armstrong, don't you? He's the principal there. He and your dad had a rather"—she cleared her throat—"interesting association with some local organizations. They weren't friends, but it might be worth looking into."

"Daddy didn't like him." Amber laughed softly at the memory. Thoughts of her father were always bittersweet.

"Landon resented that the Sons of the South rejected him." Vanessa shrugged. "I admit he's a strange duck."

"Daddy didn't belong to that, either." Amber concentrated on the spaghetti. "I don't know that he'd help me."

"That organization wanted your dad. He just didn't join. Your dad had no such ancestors. Landon did, but they actually rejected crazy Landon. Still, he and your father belonged to other organizations. It wouldn't hurt to send out your vita."

"I guess so." Amber sighed. Her head told her she had to look for employment; she couldn't rely on Winston for life. Nonetheless, she would miss her times with him as well as that very comfortable house.

"Well, Nicole said they were looking for a librarian. You should put your resume in there. Talk to them. You have two degrees, too much education to house-sit for life."

Amber nodded vaguely. *If her mother knew. . .* Maybe applying for a job was what she needed. Winston had begun to mean more to her than she wanted to admit, but she couldn't rely on him indefinitely. He was a musician with no fixed ties. He could pick up stakes at any time. She'd seek an interview at this new school.

"Mama, let's eat dinner. I don't want to talk about jobs anymore." Amber took a fork, wound a strand of spaghetti around it, and chewed happily. She was getting good at concealing her secrets.

***

Amber strode into Lakeview High School two days later armed with her vita, trying to conceal her apprehension. Unlike her previous school, this one catered to the city's elite. Like her previous job, these parents also sought to shelter their children from those considered less desirable. Landon Armstrong, the principal and her father's old nemesis, presided over a school that didn't ring bells and allowed students to roam with their salads and bottled water at lunchtime.

Nicole Smith greeted her outside the principal's office. She smiled pleasantly and said, "I'll let him know you're here." She lowered her voice but raised her eyebrows. "Between you and me, he's had a little bit this morning."

Amber steeled herself. She'd heard of Landon Armstrong when he was in his cups. Her father had laughed at Armstrong's histrionics during the meetings of the many organizations of which they were members. Any hurt, any rejection, festered like a deep wound in Armstrong's psyche. Why in hell was he drinking at ten in the morning?

Nicole said simply, "Ms. Thorpe here for your appointment." She then abruptly closed the door, scurrying away from her boss's presence.

Landon Armstrong didn't stand or offer his hand. He indicated the chair across from his desk with the regal wave of royalty greeting the masses.

Amber surreptitiously studied the room. The leather chair in which he sat was heavy. The desk was mahogany and freshly polished. Large volumes of Louisiana history graced the bookshelves on either wall. A framed portrait of his mother stared benevolently at her son. Amber knew the woman had died several years before after a life of domination over him. Rumors of fisticuffs between mother and son abounded.

Armstrong stared at her through blazing dark eyes rimmed in red. With shaking hands, he sipped black coffee from a mug boasting an image of Robert E. Lee. In a low, rusty voice, he said, "Tell me about your credentials, Ms. Thorpe."

Amber spoke about her studies in graduate school and her subsequent experience. Through her whole monologue, the man continued to stare intently at her. When she paused, Armstrong raised a regal hand. Amber waited, her hands folded primly in her lap.

"I'm sure your credentials are sound, Ms. Thorpe. I've heard good things about you through the various education channels we all have access to in this city. What concerns me is if you would be able to identify with the kind of student we have here at this school." Armstrong clasped his mug with both hands and took a shaky sip. His too-red nose disappeared into the cup as he imbibed.

Amber frowned. "I'm sorry. I'm not sure I know what you mean."

"The students here are from the cream of New Orleans society. They are Mardi Gras queens and the daughters of prominent individuals."

"Well, not all of the students at St. Elizabeth were poor or from underprivileged backgrounds." Amber had hated St. Elizabeth, but the education had not been substandard. The man's snobbery was already annoying her.

"That may be, but the students here, and their parents"—here he stressed the last phrase—"expect people who are a cut above the average educator."

"I have a master's degree. There's nothing average about that." Amber shifted uncomfortably in her chair.

"Many of my teachers and staff have that." He put his mug down with both hands, continuing in the same condescending manner. "The students here are very aware of their lineage, and your mother may come from Mardi Gras royalty. Your father, however, hails from a hippie town in Texas." His voice had risen to a shrill pitch. "That didn't stop the idiots in the Sons of the South or the Churchill Club to ask him to join. When I was in college, I wasn't doing sex, drugs, and rock 'n' roll. I was a good kid looking out for his handicapped mother."

*Who shit on you repeatedly?* Amber thought. It was the first she'd heard of the woman being handicapped. Aloud, she said, "My father didn't join the Sons of the South. He had no ancestors from that time period. Besides, he found those guys pompous snobs. As for the Churchill Club, anyone of English or Anglo-Irish background can join." Amber kept her voice steady, but she inwardly cringed, remembering her father's mocking recitation of the man's tirades.

"That may be, but I was a long member of the Children of the Sons of the South. Still those bastards shunned me, but they took your mother's cousin Paul Diaz. My lineage is better than his. Well, fuck them." He shot the bird with both hands. "As for the Churchill Club, I told them where they could get the land to build that expensive new club they're erecting. Do I get credit? No, even though I knew the people who negotiated it, and I always did my duty. Like I said, I wasn't doing the sex, drugs, and rock 'n' roll in the sixties like some of them, those hypocrites."

His voice was now a roar. He gestured wildly as he rose from his chair.

"The only reason I'm not married and don't have a wife and kids is because my fiancée hung herself in a French Quarter hotel. Some men get everything—in spite of their questionable lineage. At least your father married it. It's just a shame he had that Texas taint on his background."

Amber suppressed the urge to laugh. The man was a caricature of her father's mimicry of him. She kept her voice steady. "I'm sorry you've experienced some of this, but what does this have to do with my job application?"

Armstrong met her gaze with intensely blazing eyes. He cleared his throat in what seemed to be a vain attempt to steady his emotions. "I—I also spoke to your former employer. She revealed some things about your character that worry me—not that I trust Trish Baumann. She's a royal bitch who comes from very questionable background in Texas. Some say she's the bastard daughter of a jughead and some rural gypsy. Regardless, I know her son was the reason for a fight in the cafeteria of your—and her—precious school. Two girls fought because one reminded the other that she gave the principal's son blowjobs." He paused. "Sordid, I know, but then you know about sordid, don't you, Ms. Thorpe?"

Amber noted his swollen member inside his dark pants. Liquid from the beginning of an ejaculation had seeped onto his crotch and stained his pants. She suppressed a gag and gathered her small briefcase onto her lap.

She was now obviously genuinely angry. Blood pounded in her temples. So Trish had decided to ruin her throughout the educational community. Well, she'd get revenge.

She collected her resume and shoved it into her small satchel. "Mr. Armstrong, no one rejected you in any club because of your lineage. You actually had to hide in a closet from the FBI because of your insulting and threatening remarks aimed at a member of your own political party. People didn't want you in their clubs because you're a crazy asshole." With that, she turned and strode out.

Upon her return to the house, Amber heard Winston on the phone in the room he used as a study. At first, his voice was muffled, but then he raised it in anger and panic. She heard snatches of his end of the conversation as she crept quietly to the door.

"You should come down. It's not like that." After a brief pause, he continued, "You need to extricate yourself from that relationship. Don't make the same mistakes I did. There's a lot you don't remember." He then mumbled something she couldn't hear and slammed the phone down.

Amber rapidly made her way to the kitchen and reached into the cabinet for a bag of coffee. She placed the grounds into the coffeemaker, filled it with water, started it, and began humming. Alwena moved from her pillow in the kitchen, wagging her tail. Amber took the dog's head in her hands and rubbed her ears.

"Didn't know you were back, darling." Winston stood in the doorway, flashing that crooked smile. "Don't worry about the wee one. I took her for her walk."

Did he suspect she'd heard something? "I just walked in. Glad you and my baby are connecting." Amber reached into the refrigerator for milk and poured it into her mug. She produced another mug from the cabinet. "Would you like some?"

Winston shrugged. He said softly, "Maybe I need a pick me up. Don't put sugar in it. I need some bitterness. Make it black."

Amber understood those words. He wanted punishment, hurt, and humiliation. He wanted her to give it to him, but first, he would make those veiled confessions to her, cryptic words she only partly understood. She mechanically poured his coffee and handed him the cup.

They made their way to the living room and sat together on the sofa. Amber curled up on the comfortable cushions, her feet tucked under her. Alwena padded behind them and jumped onto the sofa. Winston sat with the coffee in his hand, staring at it.

"I wasn't always a very good father to Julian, God knows. I wasn't there for him. After his mother passed, I let my mother do the heavy lifting. At least by then my old man was gone. Old Scratch met his match. That one big heart attack took the old bastard. My mother did her best, and I did the traveling minstrel act. He resents it."

Amber nodded, taking a sip of coffee. It felt comforting sliding down her throat. There was nothing to say, but pity stirred within her.

"I tried to shelter him from what happened, but I couldn't. It was too much for us. Julian's brilliant, but he's restless. There's nothing he can't do with a computer, and he's put that to use in the military. Still, he's scarred."

Amber raised an eyebrow. "From what happened?"

Winston patted her leg. "I don't want to bore you. I've said enough."

Amber knew better than to press the issue. On more than one occasion, he'd turned vehement and almost aggressive—or, he'd dismissed her like an overly inquisitive schoolgirl. She was curious, but she understood about privacy. Hers, after all, had been wantonly invaded.

"Yes, some things should remain private. I understand. It also involves your son."

"That's right, sweet lady. Now, let's go to our special place. I need you to make me feel better." Winston stroked her arm, betraying not a hint of the terrible things he expected behind those closed doors.

Amber sighed as she made her way to that dark room, strangely titillated but frightened as well. When he unlocked the door, she stifled a gasp. The cross positioned against the wall always elicited that reaction. Today he'd removed the nails that held it to the wall. Winston moved to it, placing it in a stand very much like those that would hold Christmas trees. After securing it with a variety of screws, he turned to her.

"You know what to do, darling."

Apparently, the cage would not be used today.

Amber moved to the closet, and removed the corset and assorted accessories. Disappearing into the bathroom, she slammed the door and rapidly undressed, shedding her own jean skirt and T-shirt. She slipped into the silky stockings before sliding the corset over her body. It fit perfectly with her curves and contours.

She'd not yet retrieved the whip. That would remain in the closet until they were ready. Her heart beat rapidly; she exhaled and inhaled to still her nerves. This form of torturous pleasure repelled but thrilled her. Amber hated to admit how much she loved dominating, aggressively pursuing the sexual gratification they both needed.

Winston smiled broadly as she opened the door. He, too, had stripped down and stood before her in total nakedness. She approached him, clutched his face in her hands and pulled him to her in a rough kiss. He liked sex like this. When they made love in the easy way of sweet sex, Amber sensed Winston's soul was only halfway into the act. When they practiced hard, even sadistic sex, Amber sensed his full arousal. What frightened her somewhat was that she was beginning to respond in kind with a brutality she hadn't thought possible.

He clutched her so tightly that he bit into her lips. "Tie me to the cross, Mistress. Do your duty. Take your pleasure."

Amber retrieved the whip and knotted ropes lying at the bottom of the closet. She strode over to him, adopting the personality of seductress and vixen. It wasn't a role she'd readily accepted or wanted, but she knew what pleased him.

As she began unfastening the knots, he said, "Let's try real nails."

Amber's blood ran cold. Her voice shook and trembled within her own ears. "No, no, I can't." She shook her head, adding firmly. "No, definitely no." There was something too dangerous, too blasphemous, in this whole situation.

Winston reacted to something in the firmness of her tone. He simply nodded. "Okay. I've told you, only what you want to happen will happen. Use the ropes."

Amber moved to him. He stood on a stool and positioned himself against the cross. She tied his hands and feet tightly. His posture imitated that of Jesus perfectly. The sight sickened yet excited her. Kicking away the stool, Amber knelt before him and took him in her mouth. She sucked deeply as his moans of pleasure met her ears. Her teeth brushed against his cock a little too closely. He liked the pain. His cry was a mingling of hurt and passion. Amber stopped, looked up at him, and then stroked his member. He was passive again, awaiting her pleasure. She took him again tenderly. She couldn't hurt him for long.

"Don't make me happy, Mistress. Make me suffer." His voice was strangled with passion and what seemed to be a bizarre longing.

Amber backed away from him, moving to the closet. Retrieving the whip, she walked slowly toward him, cracking the biting leather against the shining hardwood floor. He liked the bullwhip rather than the jockey's crop. Deep scars she recognized as healed whip marks graced his legs. She smiled grimly and let loose the instrument of torture. It wrapped around his legs, breaking skin.

"Yes!" His voice was a cry. "Make me do your will, Mistress."

Amber cracked the whip again. Sprinkles of blood dotted his legs. She dropped the whip and ran to him, then stood on her toes to kiss him so hard his lips bled.

She continued to bite him as she made her way down his neck and then his chest. Amber kissed his neck and then let her lips linger on one of his nipples. When she bit him, she tasted the metallic blood in her mouth.

She ran to the chest and retrieved the crop. Slinging it along his shoulders, chest, and stomach, she began screaming, "Are you sorry yet?

Yes, you are forgiven!"

Then, Amber stroked his balls, gently at first but then with more intensity and firmness. The man groaned in a combination of agony and joy. She ran to the kitchen, returned with Cool Whip, and sprayed it on his balls and penis. She then fell to her knees and intensely sucked his growing manhood. Somehow, she had to bring something sweet from this scene of degradation and excitement, but blasphemy.

His member bulging, Winston cried out, "Take me, mistress, take me! Forgive my sins." Casting his eyes upward, he said, "Father, forgive her. She knows not what she does."

Amber thrust herself against him, the words chilling her. The cross bounced against the wall and then settled. He gave a strangled cry as she guided his member into her throbbing quim, thrusting her spine and pelvis against his hard body. She gyrated against him in rhythm, feeling the friction inside her as his body gun hardened and then erupted.

"Oh, mistress, oh, baby! Forgive me!"

The sticky evidence of his erection filled her and covered the cheeks of her vagina. She inhaled his musky, testosterone-filled scent.

Breathing heavily, Amber fell from him. She sank to the floor and curled into a fetal position. The scene was degrading, blasphemous, and frightening. Why had she succumbed? What hold did this man have on her?

"Untie me, darling." His voice was neutral now, gentle, oh so Texan and gentlemanly.

Amber rose shakily from the ground and almost stumbled toward him. She positioned the step stool at the base of the cross. With shaking hands, she began untying the ropes.

Winston dropped onto the stool and then trembling fell against her. Forcing himself upright, he gazed down at his bleeding flesh. "Excuse me while I use the facilities." He placed a hand on her shoulder to steady himself for a moment and then moved out of the room on shaky legs.

Amber called after him. "Soon, you'll have to help me atone. I may do something really evil."

\*\*\*

"Well, darling, this is a surprise." Amber always loved hearing her cousin Chuck's husky Texas drawl over the phone. She sat cross-legged on the bed, holding her address book in her hand.

"Good to hear your voice, too, Chuck! How are things in Lago Vista?"

Amber smiled as she spoke, remembering her visits to the retirement community outside Austin. Charles "Chuck" Thorpe, was her father's first cousin. He had been career military, returning home to settle in an area outside of Austin.

"Things are perfect here, sugar. Janet and I can't wait for you to visit us. We saw Aunt Margaret a few weeks ago. She said you were job hunting. Well, we got plenty of jobs in Texas." His voice sounded so much like her father's that Amber drew in a breath and stifled a sob.

"Yes, Mom and I do need to visit. We see Gran as much as we can, but we need to make the rounds on our Texas kin. We love you all." An aching began in the depths of her soul, spreading throughout her body.

"Well, what do you want to talk about, darling? Tell old Chuck." He paused, waiting.

"Did you know a Trish Baumann before you retired?" Amber held her breath. It was a pregnant question.

Amber heard Chuck pause. "Is that a marriage name?"

"Yes, her maiden name was Stevenson. I know her family was stationed at the base around Austin. Her father would probably be about—"

Chuck cut her off before she could finish. "Now, darling, I don't want to cause anyone trouble. My mama used to say if you can't say something nice—"

Amber drew in a breath before interjecting. "I know. I've heard Gran Margaret say it a hundred times. If you can't say something nice about someone, don't say it."

"It's even more complicated than that. Some of this may be violating the law for you to know this. State secrets, that sort of thing." Chuck's voice was low on the other end. He hesitated. "Why do you need to know any of this, Amber?"

Amber cleared her throat. "The woman was my principal. She fired me. I get why she had to, and I won't bore you with details. Still, she's also making it impossible for me to get a job at another school. One principal, who admittedly is an idiot, let it out that she was smearing my name."

"I see." There was a long pause. "I guess Trish has told everyone that her parents threw her out, and she lived on the streets."

"Yes, she did." Amber held her breath. She knew Chuck had made a decision to reveal something very damaging. How would she use such a revelation if it fell into her hands?

"That's not quite true. Her father deployed. Her mother was psychologically unstable. She went into a mental institution after she and Trish fought so hard one night that they both had to be admitted to the hospital with knife wounds."

Amber gasped. So the prude Trish could wield a knife. "You're kidding."

"No, I wish I were. Her father wasn't a bad guy, you know. He came back from Nam a little shaky, but he was doing his best by her and her mother. Her mother couldn't handle military life. She was abusive to Trish when old Joe deployed. Then, Janet and I did something stupid. She ran away when her father deployed, but we took her in. It was against our better judgment, and we should have followed our instincts. She stole Megan's watch. ."

"Oh no!" Amber listened, incredulous. Megan was Chuck's daughter.

"Of course, she admitted it, but we did send her on her way then. She moved in with a grandmother, but I heard she was trouble for the old lady. I lost track of her until Joe intervened and got her into the Air Force. Had anyone asked me, I'd have told them my reservations. I was Joe's friend all the way back to Nam, but that wouldn't have stopped me. Anyway, she did okay, but then disaster struck. She was sent to Afghanistan, and she met a guy who turned out to be an insurgent. Nothing was proven, but it was thought she gave him some information that led to some of our troops being compromised. If it had been proven, she could have been court-martialed and held as a traitor." He paused. "In fact, she still could be. She's still reserves." Chuck sounded sad, tired. "Remember you didn't hear any of this from me."

"Of course." Amber now had a goldmine of information on the ex-boss who was blackening her name. The question was, how she should use it? "Tell Janet and your kids hi. Love you all." With that, she pressed the button on her cell.

# Chapter Eight

## Two weeks before Christmas

Amber was in the kitchen, preparing the salad she and Winston would share with their entrée. The aroma of the roast she'd placed in the oven wafted through the house. She completed the salad, covered it, and placed it in the refrigerator. Grasping an oven mitt in her hand, she moved to the oven and stirred the ingredients surrounding her roast. Amber marveled at how much she reveled in these domestic chores and how happy she was working at her own speed. Funny, never did anyone accuse her of being domestic; however, she could really love this house and this lifestyle—at least the domestic part of it. The unorthodox aspects of her life often made her cheeks grow hot, and she blushed even brighter when she realized how easily she satisfied this mysterious man.

Alwena assumed the begging position beside her. Amber cut a piece of meat and tossed it to her. The dog's catching ability ranked with the best baseball players.

Winston was in the bedroom. She heard his soft strumming and soft singing. Was it a hymn? Then someone pounded on the door, hard. Amber started. She was expecting no one. Winston had told her no one was coming. She heard the playing stop and Winston's booted tread in the hall. Then a muffled exclamation from Winston reached her ears.

Amber emerged into the hall in time to hear Winston say, "Come in here, boy. Give your old man a hug."

Winston had grasped a much younger man in a tight bear hug. A duffel bag had been dropped at his feet. When he released the stranger, Amber immediately recognized him as Winston's son. Even though Winston was badly disfigured, traces of what must have been his once-stunning self could be found in this young man with shorn hair and piercing dark eyes. A light beard dotted his chin. With full lips and perfect skin, he was almost pretty. He smiled slightly when he saw her and nodded.

Winston turned and motioned her toward them. "Come here, darling. Meet my boy Julian." Turning to his son, he said, "I didn't think they let you grow a beard."

Julian shrugged and then held out a hand to Amber. "I've been growing it. It's got to go when I return to base, but for now, it hides the scar."

Amber didn't know what she'd been expecting, but she was stunned by the unabashed gorgeousness of Winston's son. He was as tall as his father, with very broad shoulders and a slender waist. In jeans and a long-sleeved T-shirt, Julian was obviously well-toned and muscular. His hair was the blackest ebony.

She said simply, "Nice to meet you." She couldn't, in all honesty, say, "I've heard so much about you." Winston had said very little about his son except that the younger man didn't like talking about the past. Well, neither did the father. Amber had to admit to herself that she was as curious as hell.

"Nice to meet you, too. Dad's told me a lot about you." Julian retrieved his military-issue bag from the floor and then shifted it from hand to hand.

*Had he?* Amber wondered how much the son knew of their activities in the bedroom. She felt her cheeks grow warm, but she managed a smile. This whole thing was going to be awkward. "I've been fixing dinner. Will you join us?"

"It sure smells good." Julian smiled slightly.

Alwena appeared in the hallway, wagging her tail. She trotted to the guest. Julian knelt on one knee to scratch her ears and stroke her back. He then stood with a grin. "She's a sweet little thing."

Well, he didn't sound Texan. Amber said politely, "It should be ready soon. We—we'll open a bottle of wine."

"Well, of course, she's right. She's always right." Winston slipped an arm around her shoulders. He turned to his son. "You'll stay for dinner and stay here. Let's get you into the spare room. It was yours a long time ago. Then, you can have supper with us." Winston took the bag from his son and made his way down the hallway, the younger man following dutifully.

Amber returned to the kitchen. The spare room—that in which Winston stored his computer and his guitars—had been Julian's when he was younger. Had the boy grown up here? Winston had been very vague about where he'd lived during his long years as a traveling musician, or where his mother had lived with his son. She sensed he'd lived in many places, but apparently, the son had spent considerable time here. Had his mother settled here with the boy?

Dinner brought compliments on Amber's cooking, and agonizingly polite conversation. Winston was clearly pleased to see Julian; however, they shared no family stories or anecdotes to enlighten Amber on the past. Winston kept the conversation focused on the present.

"Will you have to deploy soon or will you return to base in California?" Winston cut into his meat as he cast a glance at his son.

"Well, you know we always have to deploy. That's being a marine. But I go back to San Diego first after leave." Julian took a sip of wine. "From there, who knows? I just do as I'm told."

Amber looked from father to son. Their conversation was polite but reserved. She wondered how much of their reluctance was because of her presence. She said with a smile, "So you're a marine?"

"Semper fi, ma'am." Julian returned her smile, took a bite of food and added, "This is really good. Thanks for inviting me to stay. This beats the base grub."

Winston interjected with no shortage of pride, "Julian's a lawyer and computer geek. He talks policy and rights with the guys in places like Afghanistan and Gitmo, but he's also worn the boots on the ground, too."

Julian shrugged, colored slightly, and said modestly, "I joined before I'd finished my degree. When I first joined, my main job was carrying a gun and patrolling like everyone else." He laughed dryly, "I wanted to prove I could make it without the family money."

Winston's face darkened. There was a pregnant silence before he said, "He proved it. My boy is very decorated."

Amber smiled politely and nodded. So there was family money. No wonder Winston could support this household and another in Texas. "I see. What's your rank?"

Before his son could answer, Winston replied, "He's a major. One of the youngest."

After dinner, the three of them drank coffee and ate peach pie. Amber excused herself close to midnight and headed to bed. When she emerged from the bathroom, she heard Julian ask softly, "What does she know?"

Winston's reply was quick. "Nothing."

## Two Days Later

Amber emerged from a neighborhood dry cleaner after depositing her clothes to hear Mary Stone's voice behind her. "So I see your man's spawn has returned."

Amber slipped the ticket into her purse and kept walking as she clutched Alwena's leash. The woman repelled her. "Ms. Stone, you're stalking me, and if you don't stop this harassment, I'm calling the cops."

"So you're not the least bit curious as to why the man you call Winston Hurley is so mysterious?" Mary fell into step with Amber. Alwena emitted a soft growl. Her eyes seemed to narrow.

"No, I'm not. People have a right to their privacy. I know I sure do, and you're invading mine." Amber stopped at a pedestrian crossing, waiting for the signal. *What was taking so long?* She wanted to be rid of the woman.

When the signal flashed, Mary walked with Amber. "I'm only trying to be helpful."

"No, you're not. You want some big scoop to get in the good graces of some magazine. Well, I wish you luck, but you're not using me." Amber wished that would send the woman on her way, but it seemed to inflame her.

"Yes, well, I have heard about your, er, indiscretions and why you need to sell yourself to a fugitive and possibly his son." Mary Stone's voice was hurried, a vicious whisper.

Amber stopped walking. Pedestrians surged past them as she faced her antagonist. Some people stared at them. "I don't know what you think, but you should mind your business. Didn't you learn your lesson when every rock journal in the country dropped you? You fabricated a story—"

"I was set up. That source wanted to ruin me because I developed the idea for the logo of his magazine. He didn't want to give me credit." Mary's face went red. Her voice rose. "That's been the story of my life. I have the ideas, but no one gives me credit. Do you remember the year Lennon died? The next Mardi Gras, I gave one carnival crew the idea to put his likeness on a Mardi Gras bead. They took my idea and screwed me over. This kind of thing has happened to me here and in New York. People take my scoop and my ideas, then they discard me like trash." Mary's arms began to flail. "I did research on so many famous people, and others used my research. Do you know how much *Rolling Stone* owes me? That bitch hack Mary Ann McGuinness was having an affair with Juan DeValera, the editor for *Smoking Rock*. She would sit around with her boobs hanging out. She'd catcall me at meetings and act the bitch because she could see my attraction." Her eyes bulged huge in her head. She shook a finger at Amber. "And she could see his attraction to me."

"What does this have to do with anything?' Amber looked around helplessly. People had begun to gather and were gazing at her with a mixture of pity and curiosity. A still-life mime dressed as Joan of Arc had abandoned her pose and crossed the street, her mouth twisted in mirthful glee.

"Oh, I'll tell you! They all owe me, and your boyfriend will help me regain what they owe me. Do you know Juan actually hit me once when I was pregnant? I lost the baby." Mary's arms flailed. "And this was recent. They all continue the vendetta." Her voice gained in pitch and volume.

Amber's jaw dropped. She gaped openly. The woman had to be way over fifty. No way had she been pregnant. Alwena began barking and moved in front of Amber as if to ward off Mary.

By now, the crowd had spilled onto the street as many people stopped and stared. Some tourists paused, grinning, and yanked cell phones from purses or pockets and began filming. Others exchanged glances and hurried past. The middle-school-aged boys tap dancing on the corner giggled and rolled their eyes. By now, a police officer across the street gazed at them and made for the crosswalk, heading in their direction. Amber kept her expression passive but suppressed a laugh.

"Is everything okay, ma'am?" The cop, an earnest-looking African-American, approached Amber.

"I think this poor woman needs her medication." Amber gazed sympathetically at Mary.

"Ma'am, if you'll come with me." The officer cautiously approached Mary.

"No, I'm fine. This woman is harboring a fugitive. She may not know what she's getting into, but the man she's been with has been on the run." Mary's voice was a shrill screech. She backed away from the cop and into a gaggle of tourists who stared at her unashamedly.

The officer said gently, "Well, ma'am, I don't know about this other lady, but you're the one disturbing the peace. Come with me. No one's going to hurt you." He had the sense not to seem threatening, but Mary didn't seem comforted. She resembled an outraged goose with flapping wings and an enraged squawk.

Mary kept backing away and shaking her head. A woman wearing a scarf emerged from a nearby shop. She said kindly in heavily accented English, "Would you like to come inside with me? I have cold water in there."

Mary's eyes widened. She looked from the woman to the cop to the gathering pedestrians. The officer was talking into his radio, using some codes and obviously calling for backup.

Suddenly, sirens rang out down the street. An ambulance turned the corner and stopped by the assembled group. Two burly paramedics emerged and moved to either side of Mary. They spoke soothing words as they pinned her windmill-like arms behind her. One took a syringe from his pocket and injected the needle into her arm. Her eyes began to flutter, but she managed to say, "Do—don't believe me? You have no idea! Ask Terry Page." With that, she collapsed onto the gurney.

Amber watched as the ambulance sped away with Mary. She clearly was a nut job, but Amber's curiosity was aroused. Winston was a trifle too mysterious.

"Who was that woman?" The officer stared at Amber.

"I don't know. I've never seen her before." Amber smiled sweetly. "She just accosted me in the street." She added quickly, "And as for a man friend, well, I don't even have one, but thank you for helping me, sir."

Amber turned on her heel and walked off with Alwena. The dog was shaking her tail as if to remove an unpleasant insect. Mary may be nuts, but Amber definitely would find out who Terry Page was—online. She wouldn't ask Winston a thing.

***

Amber was on her way to Vanessa's home for an early evening chat session when she decided to detour to the public library in Lakeview near her mother's house. She made her way to the computers, removing a pen and notepad from her purse.

Typing in the name "Terry Page," she drew in a breath when hundreds of entries materialized. The woman was primarily known as the manager of Lucien Travis, the legendary guitarist; however, she'd also managed several other popular acts. She had disappeared for a time after Travis's death, apparently grieving for her friend and rumored lover. Amber printed a couple of the articles. *What in hell did that madwoman Mary Stone mean by connecting all of this to Winston Hurley?*

"Mom, what do you know about Lucien Travis?" Amber poured Vanessa and herself some wine and then sat on the sofa beside Vanessa.

"Lucien Travis? God, he's been dead now probably twenty years. Why do you ask?" Vanessa munched on popcorn from a bowl on the coffee table. At Amber's words, she choked and took a quick sip of wine. She looked down and then away. Amber sensed she was uncomfortable but didn't understand why.

"It's just that his name came up recently, a gossip rag about mysterious deaths." Amber looked at her mother over her wine glass. Amber wondered if Vanessa sensed any hidden motives, but if she did, Vanessa said nothing.

"Well, as I remember, there was mystery attached to it. His car was found, but he never was. The wife had died only a short time before." Vanessa swirled the wine in her glass. "Then, his family just disappeared." She paused. "You know, your father knew him, had played with him, even went to high school with him." Vanessa paused and then added, "I—I knew him, too, of course. Somewhat."

This time it was Amber who almost choked on the wine. "Are you kidding? Daddy knew Lucien Travis! You did, too! How did you never tell me this?"

Vanessa studied her. "I never knew you were so into music."

"Mom, come on. It's like never mentioning Paul McCartney is a relative or something. Whether you are some music aficionado or not, you brag on that connection. I never knew Daddy played with someone like that." Amber wiped her mouth with her palm, keeping her voice steady. She didn't want Vanessa suspecting her of anything. Well, what would she suspect? Amber didn't know what she herself suspected. "Besides, you know I love music. I loved hearing Daddy play."

"Your dad played in many clubs around Texas and Louisiana in his younger days. He was well-known and sought after." Her voice grew soft. "The war changed him." After a pause, she continued but looked ill at ease and shifted in her chair. "But back to Lucien Travis. Well, by then, he'd soared high. There were rumors when the wife died, you know. Some people said her death was fishy, that it was an overdose or even murder." She took another sip of wine and frowned. She looked away. "I know he was called in and questioned, but they had nothing on him. Then, he was in that accident. Delta was very beautiful, you know, but she wanted to be on the top of the world. She thought she could have everything." Vanessa's voice turned thick, bitter.

Amber swallowed and took some of the popcorn from the bowl. Why did she suspect her mother was hiding something? She avoided her mother's gaze for a long time before asking, "Wasn't there a son?"

"Yes, but no one has heard about him since his father died, at least he isn't pursuing fame and fortune." Vanessa shrugged. Amber sensed she was trying to appear indifferent but actually wasn't. "I'd met Lucien occasionally, as well as Delta, the wife, when your father played. They seemed happy, but you never know what goes on in other people's houses, do you? Like I said, she wanted it all—at least I thought so." She poured herself some more wine from the bottle on the coffee table. "Your father said something funny once about Lucien, not funny comical, but funny odd. He said that in high school many of the girls used to say he was a creative lover. He also said Delta had been a restless girl." She shrugged again. "Whatever that means. Maybe kinky stuff. I wouldn't know."

Amber's throat went dry. She'd have to investigate this more, but she also knew that she had to study videos of Lucien Travis until she knew everything about how he moved and played. Well, she'd discussed this enough with Vanessa. She cleared her throat and hoped her face hadn't grown too red. Her mother must never know about this affair. That she knew about Tyler was bad enough.

"I haven't given up sending out job applications, but it's hard when your old boss is maligning you to everybody."

"I'll rip out that woman's tongue." Vanessa's eyes were slits.

"No, Mama, don't worry about her. I think I know how to handle Trish Baumann." Amber's pulse pounded. She had to make some important decisions.

# Chapter Nine

Amber sat in front of a computer in the library on Loyola Avenue. She'd printed several articles on Lucien Travis and furtively slipped them into a manila folder. The amount of information on him was astounding: Austin-reared, Gulf War veteran, award-winning guitarist. She studied the pictures of his wife, Delta, the ultimate Mississippi belle. Lucien was handsome; Delta was beautiful. Nonetheless, their marriage had been tumultuous with rumors of infidelity on his part and hers.

Supposedly, the couple had been happy until the untimely crib death of an infant daughter. Then, the marriage slowly unraveled. They blamed each other and themselves, seeking solace outside of marriage. Their son was eight at the time of his mother's death.a handsome kid with dark hair and piercing green eyes. The boy stirred some vague memory that Amber couldn't quite identify, and Lucien reminded her of someone she knew in a subtle, disturbing way. Why did she feel as if an insect was buzzing somewhere around her subconscious?

Amber looked at the pictures. Lucien was one handsome man. He was tall and lean with a ponytail and trim beard. Dark hair, impressively muscular arms. Amber gazed at the picture of him strumming his guitar on stage, his arms flexed as he handled his instrument. The tank top accented his toned body. Like Winston, he wore some type of military medal on his cowboy hat. The picture was too blurry for her to see what kind of medal it was.

Amber scanned the articles. One was an impressive obituary of Lucien. The article portrayed him as almost saint-like, but the section on his military career was thorough and impressive. Apparently, he'd enlisted very young, escaping the repressive atmosphere in his strict, Baptist home. His father had been a preacher with very fundamentalist views who'd enforced his rules with an iron hand. Young Lucien had begun his career by playing guitar in the choir of his father's church, but the old man had forbidden his talented son to play in any blues or rock band. His music was for the Lord. Lucien hadn't listened. He'd

formed a blues band with his sweetheart, Delta, later his wife. Delta had
sung in the church choir, but she'd had a love of the blues too. When his
preacher daddy had tried to curtail his son's musical aspirations, Lucien
had joined the marines.

Amber drew in a breath. So apparently Delta also had been a singer.
What had happened to her career? As she read on, Amber found the
answer. Lucien had served almost three years in the military and fought
at the fierce Battle for Jalibah. He'd been discharged after serving his
time in the military. A lone scar marred a face that otherwise would be
labeled "pretty." Apparently, he'd been very heroic, at one time saving
several children from a burning building after a disastrous incident of
friendly fire. He'd married Delta upon his return, and they'd performed
in a band around the country until she'd had their son, Justin. The child
had been long desired, but Delta, always restless, had soon tired of her
role as homemaker.

Amber leaned back in her chair, rubbing her eyes. Okay, Lucien,
like Winston, had served in the Gulf War. Lucien, like Winston, had a
preacher for a father. As for the scar—well, Winston's face was fiercely
scarred. No one scar stood out.

She looked at a picture of him on stage at an Austin club and couldn't
contain the gasp from her lips. It was her father who shared the stage
with Lucien. Her mother had mentioned the connection, but hadn't
said that it had lasted much past high school or college. In fact, looking
back, Vanessa had seemed uncomfortable mentioning it. Then, another
picture caught her eye. Lucien had moved to the audience with his guitar,
playing to a young Delta who sat at a table, a drink in her hand. What
gave Amber a jolt was the woman sitting next to Delta—her mother
Vanessa. How deep was their connection and was Vanessa not telling
her something? She'd barely referred to Delta by her name.

"Hi, how are you?"

Amber started and quickly slid her articles in the folder. She turned
to smile into the visage of Julian Hurley. "Hi, er, good seeing you, too.
What are you doing in this part of town?"

Julian grinned at her. He was stunningly handsome in jeans and
a leather jacket. Amber wondered what he looked like in uniform.
"Checking out a book for some Christmas reading." He held up an Agatha
Christie mystery. "What are you researching?"

"I'm looking up information on jobs. I—I recently lost a job, and I'm trying to find out who's looking." Amber hoped the lie wasn't reflected on her face.

"Oh, yeah, Dad said you were a librarian." He flashed that smile again, and Amber saw traces of his father. "Well, I wish you luck."

Amber smiled broadly. The young man was affable and handsome. If he knew anything about her ill-advised relationship with Tyler, he didn't indicate any such knowledge.

"Funny, I didn't think of you as being a fan of the cozy mystery. Aren't most military guys into police procedurals or hard-boiled detective novels?"

Julian made a show of stroking the book fondly. "Now, that's a stereotype! Give me a break. You wouldn't believe how many of the guys read romances in Afghanistan. All of these book clubs sent us collected books. That stuff can get steamy." He laughed softly and then looked around. "Hey, after I check this out, would you like lunch with me? Dad's off playing somewhere until tomorrow. We can talk a little."

"Sure, why not? Let me gather up my stuff." Amber made certain that she slipped her folder into her small briefcase. No one, least of all Julian, would see her handiwork today.

Amber led Julian to a café in a nearby hotel on Poydras Street. They ordered gumbo, and Amber was amazed at how easily she could talk to him. "I hope you don't mind this comment, but you don't sound like you're from Texas."

"No, I guess not. I lived there when I was little. When my mother passed, my dad set my grandmother and me up in the digs you're house-sitting for him right now." He took a sip of his gumbo. "God, this is one thing I hate about deployment. No city has food like New Orleans." He added, with a shy smile that made him look even more boyishly charming, "Of course, no one made gumbo like my grandmother."

"Your dad doesn't say much about your mother except that you were very young when she died. I'm sorry." Amber felt a lump in her throat.

"She was very beautiful, but I don't remember much about how she died. It was a car accident, I think. All I remember is my dad telling me she'd died. Then, I stood at the funeral, holding my grandmother's hand. Then, Dad hit the road but not like he had when I was a kid." He stared in the distance, remembering. "I had the idea we were more social before, but once we moved here, people stopped visiting. The house used to be full of people, but once we left Texas, we didn't have any visitors.

I went to private schools here. My grandmother dealt with teachers, people like that. Dad never went to any school events. He'd disappear on the road for long periods. I think he wanted to forget what happened to my mother, and I think he also always fought some bad shit from the Gulf." He took a sip of iced tea. "I won't say any more. He hates to go into that kind of bullshit."

Amber shivered. What did it all mean? She forced herself to smile. "Yeah, your dad is very private."

"Well, tell me about you. Dad likes you a lot, but he's big on not discussing other people's lives. What was your life like growing up?"

Amber shrugged, keeping her expression neutral. "My upbringing was good until my dad died. I mean, he'd come home damaged by the Gulf, too, I guess. Still, he played guitar and piano," she paused, "and, by what I'm learning, knew some pretty famous people. He owned a shop that sold instruments, but he always lived close to the edge. Then, he died in a motorcycle accident." She swallowed hard. The memory still hurt. "They weren't sure it was accidental." She blinked, the tears hard to fight. "Eventually, it was ruled accidental, but our lives had to be totally rebuilt."

Why was she telling him this? The man was so damned easy to talk to. Tyler had duped her, but she sensed none of the oozing charm that had defined her ex-lover. Julian radiated sincerity, but she now had too many doubts about him, his father, and the life they lived. If it was a lie, how had they pulled it off? How much did Julian know? No one could lie that effortlessly.

"Why did you leave your other job?" Julian looked at her, his spoon poised in midair. His expression was artless.

"I—I had a conflict with my old boss. Some of it admittedly was my fault, but she had major issues with my family. I'm discovering that she may have put me in a position to screw up." She shrugged and sipped her iced tea, hoping she sounded indifferent.

"Damn! Your boss sounds like a really vindictive bitch, excuse my French." He actually blushed.

"Well, she is, but that's the thing in this whole metro area. New Orleans is one big small town. You'll meet someone who knows you or your parents or even your cousins. Someone will come up to you and say, 'I went to church with your grandparents' or 'I went to high school with your mother.' " Amber hoped her face hadn't turned scarlet as she thought of how many people she knew probably had seen Tyler's damned video.

"Yep, I see what you mean, and working in a school system makes you pretty recognizable, too, I'd imagine." Julian leaned back in his chair and rested a booted foot over his knee.

Amber noted how much like his father he was, but she merely said, "That's the truth, and right now, I'd just like to lay low. I won't bore you with details, but the last job was a bad experience."

Well, you're right. That can be hard in this town. My grandmother tried it after she came back. She'd lived here, but she wanted to keep a low profile. Still, she ran into people she knew on occasion." Julian ran a hand through his thick hair.

Amber couldn't conceal her curiosity so asked politely, "Why did she want to keep a low profile? I'm just curious. It seems like she'd want some friends after returning to town." She studied him with what she hoped was mild curiosity.

Julian shrugged. "Who knows? As I remember, my grandfather was a real no-nonsense kind of guy. He didn't put up with any BS, and I think my grandmother felt stifled. She just wanted to be alone and keep the home fires burning. Old friends made her uncomfortable, for whatever reason. When my grandfather died, I think she had the freedom to do as she pleased." He paused. "You must be angry about this ex-boss if she was so unjust."

Amber met his gaze, looked away, and then stared at him directly. "If I could find something very concrete on her, I'd do it. It's not just about me. I found out indirectly that she may be a very dangerous person."

Julian grinned at her. "Well, maybe I can help you." When Amber stared blankly at him, he simply said, "Dad mentioned that I deal a lot with technology in the military, didn't he?"

He called to the waitress and ordered two coffees. The woman wore her honey-colored hair in a ponytail. She listened to Julian with wide, appreciative blue eyes. When she had gone, he continued.

"He mentioned I was a lawyer and computer geek. I went to MIT as an undergrad. I can hack into anything."

Amber met his smile. "You couldn't jeopardize your standing in the military for me—even though this bitch was once military."

"Don't worry. I'm that good." The waitress returned with two coffees. She smiled so broadly at him that the light freckles on her face seemed to dance. Julian thanked her and poured cream into the cup. "She would never find out how you got the info."

Amber reached for the bread in a basket on the table and broke off a piece. She may have Trish Baumann in her power, but she wondered if ruining Trish would sully her own soul. But—what if Trish was dangerous, too dangerous to lead a school? Well, such concerns could wait. The photos she'd seen linking her parents to Lucien Travis perplexed her. What did or did not her mother know?

## Two days later

Amber waited at the airport terminal for Margaret to appear. The feisty Texan soon walked through the gate and into her embrace. Amber was genuinely thrilled to see her grandmother, and she luxuriated in the old woman's unabashed zest for life. Flaming curls, the color of a nighttime summer bonfire, framed her grandmother's fair skin. Snakeskin boots had replaced the traditional cowboy boots, and her trademark fur draped her small but strong body.

"How's my sweet girl? My baby granddaughter?" Margaret encircled Amber in a warm embrace that reminded her of hot fudge, warm milk laced with brandy, and late night ghost stories.

"I'm good, Gran. Mama's showing a house or else she'd be here, too." Amber returned her grandmother's embrace and then led her to the baggage claim area. "She'll meet us for dinner later, but we're going to lunch downtown." She cleared her throat. "Gran, I need to ask you some questions about my dad—and . . . and my mother."

Margaret studied her. "It sounds serious, honey. Let's have that lunch. You can ask me whatever you need to. I promise I won't avoid anything."

"Don't promise that yet, Gran, not yet." Amber headed to the door with Margaret in tow and took a deep breath.

Amber sat in Tableau, a restaurant near Jackson Square, with her grandmother and handed her the pictures as they sipped wine. "Mama never told me how well she and Daddy knew Lucien Travis and his wife. Did you know about it?"

Margaret called to the waiter. "I'll need a Red Breast on the rocks, young man." She looked hard at Amber. "What's your interest here, baby girl?"

Amber stared ahead, her gaze fixing on the waiters moving to and fro. She ran her fingertips over the rim of her wine glass. "I'm not sure. I—I've just connected with his music."

"Not sure I believe that." Margaret smiled as the waiter brought her the whiskey. "You never could fool me, girl, but that's okay. I'll let it slide for now. You're a big girl, and your business is your own"—she took a deep sip of her whiskey—"as long as you don't do anything really stupid."

Amber sighed deeply. She looked outside the long window of the restaurant. A young black man, thin as a matchstick, with a shaved head, played a plaintive blues song on a sax. A young white couple dumped some money in a hat at the musician's feet, stared in the restaurant briefly, and then moved on.

"I've already done something stupid, Gran."

Margaret raised an elegantly sculpted eyebrow. "Do you want to tell me about it?"

It was then that Amber told her grandmother about Tyler, her lost job, and meeting someone new. She deleted details of her "arrangement" with Winston Hurley but winced slightly under Margaret's scrutinizing gaze. The old woman was too sharp to fool. "Our, er, business arrangement is sustaining me while I look for a job. Honestly, Gran, I hope to be on my own feet soon."

Margaret cleared her throat and said softly. "I imagine he's not simply holding your hand, this business partner."

Amber felt the heat rise to her face. She stared ahead. A funeral party was leaving the cathedral. The limousines had pulled along St. Ann Street. The pallbearers rolled the coffin on its gurney to the hearse, lifted it, and placed it in the vehicle. A woman dressed in a black dress slipped on sunglasses as she and two teens, obviously the deceased's children, occupied the limousine behind the hearse. The sax player broke into a rendition of "Amazing Grace."

"Death," she murmured.

"What, honey?"

"Nothing, Gran, I just don't want to talk about Winston right now." Amber smiled gratefully as the waiter deposited her oyster salad in front of her.

"Winston, didn't we meet a Winston at that club?" Margaret shook her head in disbelief.

Panic raced through Amber. She didn't want to talk about Winston

Hurley, least of all in such a public place. "Please, Gran, don't. I want
to talk about Lucien Travis, not Winston Hurley." Amber's own words
made her shiver. What she suspected was absurd, almost impossible. She
slipped the articles and corresponding pictures out of her purse. "Daddy
is in some of these pictures. So is Mama. What is their connection?"

Margaret gazed down at the photos and then at Amber. Her eyes were
moist. "My John had so much talent. He could have really made it had
that godforsaken war not taken almost everything he had." She smiled
ruefully. "He and Lucien went to high school together—Davy Crockett
High, in fact. They even served together in the Gulf. The two young
fools signed up to go. They say that war was a victory, victory my ass."

Smiling through tears, she continued, "They even left UT to enlist.
Your father was such an idealist. He said it wasn't right for middle-class
kids to hide out in universities while poor people's kids died in deserts
because they couldn't afford anything else. Lucien went with him. Of
course, they were both so in love with their guitars that I thought they
would sling them across their backs on the way to the desert."

Amber attempted to concentrate on her food, taking small bites of
what was a delicious meal; however, she was held by her grandmother's
words. "So how did Lucien meet Delta or Daddy meet Mama?"

Margaret laughed slightly, her eyes taking on the luminous tint of
someone looking into the past. She daintily wiped her mouth after taking
another sip of whiskey. "Well, they both knew Delta from high school.
She was a beautiful girl. John had quite a crush on her." She spread the
napkin across her lap as the wait staff served their main courses.

"Daddy liked Delta?" Amber took this in.

"Yes, and I always felt Lucien was threatened by John's attraction
to Delta. John dated her first, but she very quickly settled on Lucien."
Margaret took a bite of her fish.

"Why do you think?" Amber leaned forward.

"Well, Lucien was driven, and I think Delta really wanted a career
for herself. She saw herself as quite a singer." Margaret nodded. "Oh,
she was good all right, but Lucien was star material. Still, there was an
attraction between John and Delta." She paused. "Well, then he met your
mother. She entered UT when he did, a genuine Louisiana magnolia.
They hit it off right away. Vanessa had what John wanted, and she
adored him. I loved her. She wasn't conceited like Delta. Then, those
murderous morons invaded Kuwait. Both those young fools enlisted."

Margaret took a deep sip of wine. "Your father came back much changed. So did Lucien, but he was all the more driven, and his career took off. Your father was wounded too badly."

"Why?"

Margaret looked down then at Amber. The tears were visible on her lashes. "Your father accidentally killed a man in his own unit over there."

Amber gasped. The waiters, patrons and bartender all seemed frozen in some still from an old-fashioned film. She clasped her fork tightly. "I never heard this before."

Margaret placed a hand over Amber's. "He wouldn't talk about it, would he? John wanted to put the past behind him, and for him, that was turning his life toward you and your mother. He shut out the past."

"Did he?" Amber clasped her grandmother's hand. "The fast cars, the motorcycles. You know as well as I do he was self-destructive."

"Vanessa tried." Margaret smiled at Amber through her tears. "He loved her and you, but we all handle our demons in different ways." She added thoughtfully, "I'm sure Lucien had his as well."

The waiter brought their coffees and dessert. Amber took a deep breath and poured cream into her coffee before speaking. Her grandmother had wiped away her tears and took a sip of coffee. "Gran, did he keep in touch with Lucien?'

"Yes, Lucien didn't forget a friend. In fact, he and your father had played at an Austin club the weekend Delta died."

"I see." Amber took a sip of coffee to suppress the chill that raced through her. She cut into her cake and smiled at her grandmother. "Let's talk about other things."

After depositing Margaret at Vanessa's house, Amber glanced at her phone. Yet another school had rejected her application. Well, it had been quite a day. She had questions for her mother, but those would have to wait. She had to take care of the threat Trish Baumann posed. But how?

## The next day

"Is it all right if I borrow Julian later today?" Amber looked at the father and then the son. They sat together at the table eating a breakfast of fruit and pancakes. She turned to Julian. "Is it okay with you?"

"At your service, ma'am." Julian grinned at her and gave a mock salute.

"I may need some computer help."

"Well, he's a wiz at that." Winston couldn't hide the pride in his voice. "My boy can hack into anything." He patted his son on the shoulder.

"You're exaggerating, but I know how to find things some people can't." Julian blushed and looked down. He concentrated on his breakfast and cut into his pancakes.

Later that day, Amber sat with him on the sofa in the living room while a fire blazed. Alwena sat beside her, her head resting comfortably in Amber's lap. Julian had retrieved his own computer from his belongings and turned it on.

"I know how to work this baby. Besides, it contains certain codes I can use to find out what you need. Nobody will track me on here. You just can't say where you got it."

"I won't." Amber crossed her heart. "Promise."

"I'm not going to ask what you're going to do with it." Julian looked at her, studying her closely. He was handsome; she could see traces of his father in him—the way he moved, how his muscles flexed. He also reminded her of someone else, but she pushed that to the back of her mind. His fingers moved over the keyboard. "Give me this person's name and branch of service." He paused. "It is someone in the military you want to know about, right?"

Why did his presence ignite such a torch in the depths of her stomach? Amber felt her face grow hot. She'd been around other handsome men. She'd given herself to others, including his father. Instinctively, she moved nearer to him, drawn by an attraction that sparked something like molten lava in the depths of her soul. He placed a hand over hers. Then, as if by mutual accord, they looked away from each other and drew apart.

Amber gave him Trish's maiden and married names. Her own voice sounded stifled in her throat. She turned from him while he typed in passwords and codes so secret that seeing them might violate government law. While he worked, Julian made no comment. Then, he said, "It's printing in the other room."

Amber raced to the printer Winston had set up in the study. Alwena barked after her.

Winston sat on a chair, playing his guitar. "I take it Julian was able to help you."

Amber clasped the printout in her hands and read over it. "I think so."

"You know, darling, sometimes you don't always wind up loving what you wished for." Winston looked up from his guitar. An ambulance siren wailed outside while the vehicle roared up the street. Winston cast a careless glance at the window. "Some poor sod probably going to meet his maker."

"I—I need to see Julian about some of this. It's Greek to me." Amber ran her tongue over her lips and raced from the room. She'd feel recrimination for ruining Trish another time.

"What does it mean?" Amber sat with Julian, too close to him, staring at the file on her former boss. Their shoulders touched as she looked over him. Alwena joined them, staring at the documents as if reading them.

Julian looked hard at the document, his brow creased deeply. "Your friend is a traitor, but the military couldn't quite prove it." He pointed to a line in the document. "She received a general discharge because they didn't have enough on her to court-martial and label her 'dishonorable.' Still, she did compromise troops and sold her soul for a good fuck." He turned red and said quickly, "Excuse my French."

Amber hoped she concealed her delight. Some neighborhood kids walked along the sidewalk outside, rapping and blasting a radio. She cleared her throat. This was too good to be true.

"What exactly did she do?"

"Your friend Trish was quite the little IT wiz herself while she did her stint in the air force , but she met up with a national when she went to Afghanistan. Apparently, the guy was acting as an interpreter for the armed forces over there. Let's just say he wasn't what he was supposed to be. Your girl spilled her guts to him while they were in the sack." He pointed to the document.

"Did she mean to do it?" Amber's gaze flew over the document. No wonder Trish had no soul. She'd sold it to the devil. "Or was she just some lovestruck idiot?"

Julian again indicated the document. "That's why she wasn't convicted and sent to prison. They couldn't prove her actions had been purposeful. Her military lawyer argued she was a misled young woman, but the prosecutor didn't buy it. His argument is pretty convincing, but the jury was hung. She was discharged, tail between her legs, but no actual criminal record." He looked at Amber. "She could have been tried and thrown in jail. It's only because she had a good lawyer she wasn't."

"Are you that good a lawyer?" Amber smiled at him.

"I like to think so, ma'am." Julian returned her smile and winked at her. "Take it. Do what you will." He closed his laptop and stared intently at her.

Amber felt her blood grow warm inside her veins. "I won't say where—"

"Don't worry. I blotted out any evidence of where it originated." His hand lightly touched Amber's as he handed her the pages.

Amber clutched the papers in her hand. She moved closer to him, their lips too close. Alwena growled softly. The door down the hall opened, and as if by mutual accord, they jumped apart. Amber quickly slipped the pages into a folder.

### The next day

Amber made her way to the library in Lakeview and made copies of the documents Julian had retrieved. She then drove to the post office where she mailed them to the archdiocese and superintendent of schools. Afterward, she made her way to her mother's home with Alwena looking out of the windows from the back seat. Margaret had gone to visit an old friend, and Vanessa had invited Amber to dinner.

"Why didn't you tell me you and Daddy were so tight with Lucien Travis? That Daddy actually dated Delta Travis?" Amber carried the plates to the table. She set the table while her mother brought the food into the dining room. Alwena had already taken a place on the floor by the table where she could best beg food from both women.

Vanessa studied her, a bowl of vegetables in her hand. She placed it squarely in the middle of the table and balled up the kitchen towels she'd used to clasp the dish. "Gran told you this, right? Well, she can exaggerate sometimes."

"I don't think she did." Amber poured wine into their glasses. She pushed the cork back into the bottle and stared at her mother.

"Maybe I don't like remembering the past. After all, everyone associated with that time is dead—except me." Vanessa stressed the last part of the sentence. "Remembering pleasant times can be painful when those times are past." She disappeared into the kitchen.

"I understand that, but you seem uncomfortable even when I mention Lucien Travis's music." Amber followed her into the kitchen and stood opposite Vanessa, her fists on her hips.

"Let's eat." Vanessa slipped past her and into the living room.

"Did you not like Lucien and his wife for some reason?" Amber followed her mother to the dining room table. When Vanessa avoided her gaze, Amber pressed it. "Was Daddy involved with Delta?"

Vanessa sat at the table and spread the napkin over her lap. "Sit down and eat." When Amber complied, she continued, "I'll say this. Years ago, your father was involved with Delta. That ended when she met Lucien. Then, your father met me, but he always remembered her fondly." A bird chirped outside. Vanessa said softly, "Maybe I was jealous and didn't want to admit it."

Amber sipped her wine. "What was she like?"

"Delta? Pretty but driven. She wanted a man who would make it big, and that was Lucien. He was chasing the dream." Vanessa shook her head. "Your dad wanted more of a stable family life for you."

Amber felt the lump grow in her throat. "He was pretty reckless, Mama. The motorcycles . . ." Her voice trailed away.

"Yes, but that side of your father only came out after the Gulf. John was always gentle, kind. Lucien was a good guy, but he wanted to be big time." Vanessa added quickly, "Of course, they still played gigs together. You know, John and I were there the weekend Delta died."

Amber's pulse quickened. "How did she die, exactly?"

"She fell down the stairs. Broke her neck. It was tragic. We didn't say a lot about it. Lucien called us from the hospital. It was terrible, and the boy was hysterical. In shock." Vanessa studied her plate. "Let's eat and not talk about unpleasant things. Let's talk about Christmas. Will you be spending it with us? This new employer can come to dinner, too, you know." She looked down at her plate. "Those were grand times for a while. Losing all of that hurt."

Amber nodded and smiled faintly. She speared a vegetable with her fork. "Well, he's going to California. His son has to report back to base soon after. They're spending quality time together."

Winston had told her about his coming departure. Amber was going to miss him, and a part of her admitted that she would miss Julian even more.

Why did she feel Vanessa's explanation lacked something? Honesty? Sincerity? Outside, an ambulance careened down the street, its siren blaring.

# Chapter Ten

"No, I didn't see the newspapers yet, and I fell asleep before the news." Amber sat across from Jen Brocato, eating lunch at Maspero's on Canal Street.

"It was in the Metro section. The archdiocese fired Trish." Jen tore a sugar pack apart and shook it into her iced tea. Her long, black hair was in its trademark ponytail, and she gazed at the world with dark, innocent eyes. She would have been attractive had she accented her Italian features with any makeup or fashionable clothing; however, her mother and grandmother had inculcated notions of modesty and propriety out of date in a modern society. Amber knew she'd die of horror had she known of Amber's relationship with Winston Hurley.

Amber squealed with delight at the news. Clapping her hands together, she said, "Did they give any explanation? The papers, I mean."

"Somehow the papers had all of this information on her military record. The archdiocese was confronted with some information about her past. They let her go to avoid a scandal." Jen frowned and cut her catfish po'boy in half. "How would the paper get that kind of stuff?"

Amber shrugged. She wasn't about to tell her naïve friend her role in Trish's downfall, but Amber hadn't sent anything into the newspapers. Had Julian? Winston? Jen was too honest by half, but she did teach math at the school.

Amber grilled her on the reaction to Trish's downfall. "What happened? Did she come and say goodbye?"

"No, we got there the morning after the story, and her door was locked. She didn't even come in. I hear her son is going right into the military after graduation. They can't afford college for him." Jen looked across at Amber. "Do you think she'll find another job?"

Amber bit into a French fry. She winked at Jen. "Who knows? Most places don't want to hire a traitor."

Jen stared at her. "You said you didn't see the papers."

"Yeah, so?"

"How did you know they accused her of being a traitor? I didn't tell you that yet." Jen looked away, took a bottle of mustard, and spread it on her sandwich. "At least they tried. They couldn't really prove it."

Amber hoped her face wasn't turning red. "I—I just guessed. After all, how else do you get into trouble in the military?"

Jen said nothing. The man with the sax who Amber had seen earlier blew his horn on the corner. The tune was plaintive, sorrowful. Amber looked at him. He met her gaze and continued playing. His eyes were large and deep, and held a hard sadness that made Amber shiver.

That night, Amber sat on the sofa next to Winston sipping red wine. "When do you and Julian leave for California?"

"In two days, but we have some time before then, darling." Winston winked at her.

"Where is he tonight, by the way?" Amber kept her voice neutral, but she enjoyed Julian's presence at dinner. She hated admitting how much she would miss him when he permanently returned to duty.

"Julian went to school here. He still has some friends in town he occasionally sees." Winston studied her over his wine glass. "Why do you ask?"

Amber took a sip of wine and shrugged. "Just wondered. I hope I fixed enough for dinner."

Winston grinned and winked at her. "You always do, darling."

"I—I also wanted some privacy tonight for us." Amber slowed down, gathering her thoughts. "I did something I really am not very comfortable discussing, but I—I want you to punish me." The last words came out too quickly. She looked away, feeling the heat rise in her cheeks. "It's something I thought would make me happy, but it's made me see a side of myself I don't always like."

Winston's expression held no judgment. He indicated the hallway. "So you want the back room? Maybe even the cross?"

A chill ran up Amber's spine. She shook her head. "No, not the cross. I'm not ready for it, and I don't know that I'll ever be."

Winston nodded and drained his wine. He lightly touched her leg. "I can see that. You're a good Catholic girl. That whole idea must horrify you."

"It does, to be honest, but I do need punishment. I've done something that's not quite honest." Amber looked at a copy of a Degas on the wall. The bells at the cathedral chimed.

"About us?" Winston's tone remained noncommittal, but he stroked her bare leg.

"No, someone who wronged me at work. I did something underhanded to get even." Amber didn't add that she'd enlisted his son to help her ruin someone's life. In fact, she wasn't sure how he would react to her making Julian a companion or confederate.

"We do what we have to." Winston studied her and then stood slowly. "I'll ready the room. You can get into your clothes."

Amber removed the submissive's clothing from her own closet, dodged into the restroom and removed her clothes. She examined her body in the mirror. She was growing thinner, more toned and conscious of her figure. She slipped into the black bikini slowly, running a hand along the embroidered white flowers along the bust and pubic mound. She was a paid whore; she had no illusions. Her "house-sitting" was a ruse for other paid services. How had she come to this?

Somewhere in this maze of deceit she had decided not to question where this whole scenario had led her. School librarian to paid submissive. Well, she was living in style, frequenting restaurants and establishments she wouldn't have afforded on her librarian's salary. There were worse fates, but Amber knew in her heart's core that she couldn't maintain this lifestyle. Winston would move on. She wasn't his first "mistress" or "submissive." Another woman had stepped into those clothes before her. And what she couldn't deny was her growing attraction to Julian. His devastatingly handsome good looks were only part of what made her heart race like a marathon runner. She loved his smile and the genuine nature she saw underneath a demeanor that was at first guarded.

Besides, Amber sensed she was on the tip of a tall volcano about to spew lava. How much Julian knew of his past was uncertain, but Mary Stone was only partly insane. There was some truth to her insane ramblings. Amber knew it. Winston wasn't what he appeared to be, but whether he was Lucien Travis or not was another matter. By what she'd read, conspiracies about Lucien's death had run rampant. Nobody wanted to admit that the talented guitarist was dead, but Amber, too, had begun to wonder if those "conspiracy theorists" were altogether wrong. She's studied the videos of Travis playing on YouTube. He was brilliant, and Winston's playing was very like his. Still—could this man so scarred be the same person, and was he capable of the kind of subterfuge that had lasted over twenty years? Who could sustain such a lie?

Well, Amber was about to walk into their secret room and give herself over to a man who definitely was not what he seemed. Did she enjoy the thrill? The subterfuge? Perhaps the deceit was part of the thrill.

As she gingerly pushed open the door, Amber saw the cage looming ahead. Winston stood beside it, a whip in his hand. He wore a Lone Ranger–type mask and a black cowboy hat with studs. Black leather pants with spikes hugged his hips, and he cracked the whip on the ground when he saw her.

"Move to the cage, darling."

The accent was so gentlemanly, so charming. Candles, positioned around the cage, lit the dark expanse of the room and cast ghostly shadows across his scarred face. Amber stepped inside. Handcuffs were already attached to the bars of the cage. He'd spread hay around the floor of the cage. *A fitting metaphor*, Amber thought. *We are the animals here.*

When she closed the door, Winston stepped near her and said softly, "Inside the cage."

Amber nodded slightly and swallowed. She walked through the open door. What had it been designed to hold? A monkey? An ape? A horse, even? The hay crunched under her bare feet. Passively, Amber let Winston take her wrists in his and cuff her to the cage. After she was secured, he knelt and secured her ankles. She was totally helpless and under his control.

Winston unfurled the whip and cracked it against her bare thighs. She winced and bit her lip, willing herself not to cry out. Abruptly, without warning, Winston pulled her head back and kissed her hard on the mouth, forcing his tongue into her clenched lips. She still winced from the whip and suppressed a cry when he forced her mouth open. The skin on her legs wasn't broken, but the imprint of the whip marked her legs and stung. The cuffs cut into her wrists and ankles as Winston moved from her mouth to her neck, his tongue running across her flesh and then sucking her hard. When his lips wrapped around her nipples, he bit into her skin until she couldn't suppress a cry. She was suspended against the cage bars, her breath coming fast as he ran a finger down her bikini bottom, feeling the hair on her mound.

Abruptly, Winston released her wrists, dropping the whip and reaching into his pants pocket to extricate the key and unlocking her so that she fell into his arms. He then knelt and unlocked her ankles. Amber held onto his shoulders, leaning forward until he righted her. Then, he commanded her harshly. "On your knees, woman."

Her wrists and ankles aching, Amber fell to her knees as Winston unzipped the tight-fitting pants. His member bulged in his briefs. Amber gazed up at him and then pulled the underpants down. Winston stepped out of the briefs and pants.

"You know what to do."

Amber moved closer to him, stroking his cock, and then took him in her mouth. She sucked deeply, feeling him grow inside her. His soft moans of pleasure resonated in her subconscious as she subtly withdrew from him, gazing upward.

"On your hands and knees." His voice was husky, catching in his throat. "Do you want to be ridden?"

Amber let him blindfold her with a cloth he had tied to the bars. The hay was hard and itchy against the palms of her hands and her knees. He grasped her hair, pulling it backward as he straddled her, thrusting against her. When he entered her, Amber cried out from the force of his penetration. Releasing her hair, Winston leaned backward and struck her ass, hard, repeatedly. He thrust so deeply and struck so hard that Amber ached, screaming, "Hurt me! Punish me!" As her cries grew more impassioned, Winston exploded inside her, sending his warm flowing lava between her soft sex.

Amber collapsed under him, rolling onto her back. Panting heavily, she gazed up at him. He stood over her, extending a hand. Sweat gleamed from his toned body. "Come on, darling. You've suffered enough. Time for bed."

Later that night, Amber lay in his arms as he stroked her bare breasts. They shared a flask of whiskey until it was gone. Then, Winston rubbed her sore body in lotion, gently massaging her wrists and ankles. When Winston left the room briefly, Amber buried her face in the pillow and wept softly until she fell asleep.

## The next day

Amber watched Winston and Julian leave for the airport in the early morning hours. Julian barely looked at her, uttering the quietest of goodbyes. Winston's fatherly kiss was almost as innocent. Father and son had petted Alwena until her tail wagged with delight.

Amber waved as their hired car pulled away and then retreated up the few steps leading to the house with Alwena at her heels. She fixed coffee and imbibed it slowly. She was going to miss Winston, but she had to admit to herself that she would miss his son even more. The brief time they'd spent together had meant more than she would admit. A bond had grown between them, but here she was at Christmas, without the father or the son. Well, she and Vanessa were leaving themselves, heading to Texas to visit Margaret. Alwena would board with the groomer.

Amber always loved seeing her grandmother, but she felt a hole in her own heart. It wasn't that her relationship with Winston was obscene and transient; it was the fact that Amber wanted someone in her life who loved her and whose love she could return with true devotion. She didn't have that with Winston. Could she have that with Julian? She sensed his attraction. It was real, she knew. Amber wanted that attraction to grow, but she'd suffered betrayal already at Tyler's hands. She didn't want a repeat of that situation and knew that this relationship with Winston could only lead to disaster.

Amber made for the bedroom, retrieving her purse. When she unzipped the bag to retrieve her keys, she found the letter:

*Dear Amber,*

*I'm spending Christmas Day with Dad at the base, but I can get away two days later. He's engaged in some business crap for a few days. I know a place in San Francisco where we can meet. It's very close to the ocean and very private. My instincts tell me you feel the same as I do, and I want you for myself those days. You might think I'm a real bastard for moving in on Dad, but my feelings won't go away. I've tried keeping thoughts of you from my mind, but I can't do it. Do you feel the same? Don't we owe it to ourselves to see if what we have is real?*

*Julian*

Amber gazed at the letter, mixed emotions racing through her. Julian had provided the name of the hotel and the address under his signature. The Seal Rock Inn, Point Lobos, San Francisco. Her heart raced like that of a bird caught in a web. He did feel as she did, and that fact filled her with pulsating excitement as well as an almost paralyzing trepidation. Tyler had betrayed her with a friend; he'd used their intimate encounters together to ruin her life. Yet here she was, contemplating betraying Winston with his own son. What did this make her? For that matter, what did the whole part she'd been playing make her, and why was she playing it?

Throughout her life, Amber had never been a superstar. Though she'd done well in graduate school, she'd never received the grants or awards some of her peers had. When she'd joined the faculty at her high school, she'd been respected (at least until Trish arrived), but she'd never been the favorite. Amber never understood it. She performed her duties well; she was friendly but professional with everyone. Still, others were promoted over her. Even when she worked for the degree in professional leadership, someone else became vice-principal of academics. Well, by then, Trish had arrived and hated Amber and everything associated with her family.

Maybe she enjoyed the sexual power she knew she held. Still, how could she betray a man with his own son? What did that say about her or about Julian? Amber stood with the letter in her hand and knew she would meet him—even though she felt like a Judas.

Wait! How would she reach him? Oh, she did have his cell number. She grasped the phone from her purse and ran her tongue over her dry lips. She wiped the sweat from her palms. Then, suspicion raced through her. What if this was a trap on the part of the father and the son to trick her and reveal her true character? Well, Amber wondered about her true character as well. Brushing aside her doubts as she pushed back a stray hair from her face, she texted Julian.

> I'll be there.

His response was simple.

The screen was filled with kisses.

# Chapter Eleven

Amber and Vanessa arrived at Margaret's home in Austin on Christmas Eve, attended Midnight Mass with her, and then helped her prepare dinner for assorted family the next day. Amber enjoyed the time with her grandmother and paternal relatives. They all represented the good times she'd had with her father, and Amber desperately wanted to hold onto the good memories of John.

"Oh, Cousin Chuck will be here shortly." Margaret wiped her hands on a dish towel.

"Oh, good. I don't see them enough." Amber looked up from her work at the kitchen table. She was mixing mayonnaise into the potato salad and reached for the cloth her grandmother extended to her. It was Christmas Day, and the brisk weather invigorated her, filling her with excitement. Still, she sensed that recent events would forever alter the path on which she'd embarked.

"Chuck sounded very mysterious. He mentioned something about having news for you." Margaret pulled up the chair opposite Amber.

Amber shrugged, maintaining a neutral expression. "Well, I did talk to him recently about a mutual friend."

"Well, it seems as if he has some news about that person." Margaret studied Amber and then took her hand. "You don't seem at ease, girl. What's wrong? How does that employer treat you?"

"He's very generous. All I do is sit in his house and do some cleaning. He plays me well." Amber gingerly freed her hand and went back to her potato salad.

"Is there more to the relationship? I've asked before, I know. Be honest." Margaret raised an eyebrow and gazed at Amber appraisingly.

Amber never could withstand her grandmother's withering stare. She shrugged. "I don't know. Frankly, I'm not sure if I'm attracted to him or his son."

"His son?" Margaret frowned but her eyes held some amusement. "My, I didn't know my very prim librarian granddaughter got around so much."

Amber felt the heat rise in her face. "I—I can't go into it, Gran. There are some things I just can't say."

Margaret nodded. "Understood. Sometimes, silence is best." She sighed and moved to the cabinet to retrieve the wine glasses.

Amber cleared her throat. Why was her heart pounding so loudly? Why did she think this moment would change something in her future? "Gran, exactly how well did you know Lucien Travis? You told me some things but not all."

"I knew Lucien well. He and your father were very good friends as young men. Lucien came to the house often. He was always a very polite young man. That Delta was gorgeous but destructive." Margaret smiled at Amber. "Would you like a glass of wine while we work?"

Margaret moved to the cabinet and removed a bottle of red wine and two glasses. She poured two liberal amounts of wine into each glass. She then removed French bread from the kitchen counter, sat across from Amber, and began cutting the loaf.

"His death was sad. Delta died in that horrible accident." Margaret shook her head. "Funny, I've thought about him quite a bit lately. I think it was seeing that guitarist at the club when you were here, now your boss."

Amber looked up at her grandmother, startled. She kept her voice neutral. "How did you know I was working for Winston?"

Her grandmother chuckled. "I'm not stupid, my girl." She continued, "Something about Winston's voice, and of course, his guitar-playing is magnetic. Few people can do what he can. Your father was brilliant, but he was talented in all areas. With Lucien, the guitar was everything. It was the center of his existence. There were all kinds of rumors when he died. Some people say he never died. After all, they never found his body." She shrugged. "Who knows? Delta's death was horrible for everyone. Your mother and father were visiting then. They were at the house when she had the accident. That Austin guitarist is sure like him."

Amber suppressed a gasp. She kept her voice neutral. "None of the papers said they were there. Mama mentioned it, but she was evasive." What news would her grandmother reveal?

Margaret looked at her curiously. "I didn't know you were so interested in Lucien Travis."

"I—I—" Amber's mind raced. She said quickly, "When I heard Daddy knew him, I wanted to know more." She felt the moisture gathering in her eyes. A gaping pit opened within her soul. "I miss him so much."

"So do I, honey. So do I." Margaret bit her lip and patted Amber's hand.

It was then the doorbell rang and Amber moved down the hall to the door to answer it. Chuck, his wife Janet, and their children arrived. Megan's fiancé Mason, also military, arrived in tow. Amber embraced Chuck and each family member in turn. She'd forgotten how like her father Chuck was—tall and dark-haired with the same startling green eyes.

"I suppose your grandmother mentioned that I had news for you." Chuck winked at her after he'd placed gifts under the tree.

"She did mention it." Amber was curious; however, she didn't want the mention of Trish Baumann's name sullying the holiday.

"Well, the military discovered new evidence to prosecute Trish. Someone uncovered evidence and sent it to the military. Military police took her into custody on Christmas Eve. It hasn't been in the papers yet, probably tomorrow." Chuck followed Amber into the kitchen.

Amber poured him some wine into a glass on the table and handed it to him. She swallowed. Had Julian come to her rescue? "Do they know how this information was obtained?"

Chuck shrugged. "My contact didn't say. He's pretty up on things, but he had no knowledge of how the military came by this. They're pretty tight-lipped about it. The brass find it embarrassing when one of our own is actually a rat." He took a sip of wine. "I feel bad for her in some ways, but Trish brought this on herself. The military was her salvation. They took her in when she had nobody, and she betrayed them. Just like she did her father—talking trash about him and having no compassion for her mother."

"Not to mention what you and Janet did for her." Amber saw the hurt in her cousin's eyes. Trish had walked over everyone, but she was now going to feel the effects of her treachery. "I, well, I just don't like being anyone's downfall."

"Don't feel bad. You couldn't have found out the stuff the military now has on her." He patted her arm. "Besides, you did a service to your country. Many young people died because of her."

Christmas dinner was boisterous with the arrival of still other relatives. Margaret's sister Peggy arrived in her trademark Beatle boots, even though she now needed a cane, and bore a gift of rare bourbon. Her daughter Myra brought a huge Santa Claus wreath that was cheery but gaudy. Margaret loved it and hung it on the front door immediately.

The relatives reminisced at dinner. Peggy took a sip of straight bourbon and sighed deeply. She said, "My Lord, Amber, you sure look like your daddy. Your hair's not as dark, but you have that amazing John smile and those gorgeous eyes." She turned to Vanessa. "And you're a beauty, too, young lady. No surprise you and John made a beautiful baby."

Myra, blond curls framing her face, questioned, "Do you play guitar, Amber?"

Amber shook her head, smiling. "I'm afraid I didn't get my father's musical genes."

"Well, he was a genius on the guitar, and when he played with Lucien Travis, it was magic." Myra buttered a sweet roll.

Amber continued smiling but noticed her mother stiffen. Did her seeming discomfort derive from memories of her husband, or did the mention of Lucien Travis make her uneasy? Amber knew she had to question Vanessa about Delta Travis's death, but she didn't think Christmas dinner was the right time. No, any hard questions had to wait until tomorrow.

Amber finished packing for San Francisco before she confronted her mother. Vanessa was in the kitchen, seated at the table, a coffee cup in her hand. She smiled at Amber. "I'm not going to ask why you have to leave so early, but I'm disappointed. I'm sure Margaret is, too."

"I'll be back for New Year's Eve." Amber moved to the sink and poured a cup of coffee from the bubbling pot. "I'm visiting a friend I haven't seen in a long time." Amber avoided Vanessa's gaze. It wasn't quite a lie. It seemed ages since she'd seen Julian, and she was running to him not knowing what the future held. In all likelihood, she would be in his bed. Wasn't she betraying Winston with his son? Still, if what Amber suspected was true, Winston had betrayed countless people. What exactly did her mother know?

She turned to Vanessa, blew on the steaming coffee, and attempted to sound indifferent. "You never told me the details about the night Lucien Travis died, not really."

Vanessa visibly stiffened. She looked at Amber through narrowed eyes. "It wasn't a pleasant time. Delta's death was traumatic. I don't want to talk about it. Besides, we were only called after the fact."

"It's more than that, Mama. You know it. What happened the night Delta died? Why were you and Dad there? Was it a friendly visit when she died? You and Daddy were visiting, having a glass of wine, and Delta just fell down the stairs?" Amber phrased it as a question and tried to keep her voice steady.

Vanessa slammed the cup on the table. "What are you implying? I can read you, Amber. Besides, as I said, we weren't at the house at the time, only later."

"The way she died was suspicious, that's all." Amber moved to the table, pulled out a chair, and sat beside Vanessa. "I—I've been reading a lot about that time and wanted to know more." She gazed at her mother. What was she so afraid of?

"What's the use in digging up the past? Winston and Delta are dead. Your father, God rest him, is gone, too. I've seen enough of death from people too young to go. Why read about someone who died such a terrible death?"

"Was Delta's death an accident?" Amber ran a hand over her coffee cup and looked down. She couldn't look at her mother when she posed that question. Her heart beat like the drum in a school band. What did she want of Vanessa?

Vanessa's eyes widened. She stuttered and grasped Amber's hand. "Of course. What else would it be?"

"Did you see it? Be honest." Amber pulled her hand from Vanessa, gesturing wildly. "How do you know it was an accident?"

Vanessa shook her head vigorously. "No, I didn't see it. Your father and I were not there at the time. We'd stayed in Austin that weekend. John and Lucien had a gig. Lucien called us, frantic. When we got there, police and EMTs were already there. Her neck was broken. She was dead."

Amber studied her mother. She sensed Vanessa wasn't telling the whole story. "Was her son there, too?"

"Why all these questions? You'd think you personally knew them. I did, and remembering this isn't pleasant." Vanessa stood abruptly, moved to the sink, dumped out her coffee, and made her way to the liquor cabinet. She opened the glass door and poured whiskey into her cup. She took a deep swallow before continuing. "You were a baby. John had played a gig with Lucien. We'd left you with your grandmother.

It was going to be a casual night with friends. We were having a good night at the club. Then, we went back to Gran's. I honestly don't know how Delta fell."

"Was she drunk?" Amber saw her mother's pain but pushed on.

"No, she wasn't." Vanessa rinsed out her cup. "Look, I've had enough of the Q & A." She made for the door but stopped. "And I know about your boss. It's that guitarist we met here." Her voice caught. "You'd better be careful."

Amber gasped. "How did you know?"

Vanessa ignored the question. "Just call me when you arrive in San Francisco. I worry about you." She slammed the door.

Amber stared after her. Was that all Vanessa knew of the night Delta died? Why did she think her mother was purposefully evasive?

### The next day

Amber landed in the Oakland Airport late that afternoon, rented a car, and drove to San Francisco with the help of a sophisticated GPS. She checked into the Seal Rock Hotel, a boutique hotel located very near the ocean. The cold air invigorated Amber as she collected her bag from the trunk and pushed open the door.

A tall, young Asian man smiled at her, raising a quizzical eyebrow. "Checking in?"

"Yes, I think my friend is already here. Julian Hurley." Amber shoved her shoulders out of the sweater.

The clerk produced a key. "Mr. Hurley said you should make yourself comfortable. He should be back soon."

Amber made her way to the second floor and opened the door. Julian had lit the fireplace, which blazed, warming and lighting the room. The refrigerator contained a bottle of wine and a covered box. Wine glasses graced a small end table. Amber unpacked the few items she'd brought, moved to the bathroom, and brushed her hair. It was then she heard the door open.

"You look lovely in spite of the long flight." Julian ran a hand over his crew cut, smiling almost shyly. He was clean-shaven. A faded scar marred his chin.

"It—it wasn't that long." Amber's throat went dry. She swallowed hard. He looked unbelievably handsome in jeans, cowboy boots and a marine T-shirt.

"Are you up for a walk along Land's End and then a Bloody Mary at the Cliff House? The restaurants there are good." Julian's smile broadened and grew more desirous. "We can come back here later."

"What about the wine in the fridge?" Amber found herself smiling. A tingling formed in the pit of her stomach. No one had a right to be so handsome.

"We're not limited to one type of drink." Julian crossed over the threshold to place a light hand on her face. "We have the next two days to do all sorts of things."

Amber felt her face grow hot. She ran her tongue over her lips and touched his hand. "What's in the box in the refrigerator?"

"A surprise for you." Julian paused significantly. "After we have some dinner. I'm buying."

Amber slipped on comfortable walking shoes and a woolen sweater. She looked at Julian in the leather jacket he'd donned, and her blood burned hot with desire. "I hope the Bloody Marys are good and the service is quick. I don't like waiting for good things." She met his gaze as he opened the door.

Julian laughed, throwing back his head. He drew near to her. "You are such an enigma."

"Am I?" Amber raised an eyebrow.

"On the surface, you seem to be a very prim librarian, albeit a pretty one." He paused, his gaze running over her body.

"And I'm not?" Amber grinned. She moved closer to him, letting her face touch his. His breath featured her hair.

"You are all sensuality under that prim exterior. All passion, all madness." Julian took her hand, moved closer, and ran his lips over her fingers. "We could take the walk later. Even the Bloody Mary could wait."

Amber sighed deeply, clutching his hand and letting him lead her into the depths of the room. She rested her cheek against his. "Where are we going with this?"

"I tried denying you. I didn't want to go anywhere near what my dad does, but I can't deny how I feel." Julian moved to the refrigerator, removed the box, and placed it in the microwave. He then strode over to her, planting a hard kiss on her lips. "I want you. I can't help it."

Amber melted into his arms, clutching him around the waist as he pushed her onto the bed while lifting her sweater over her shoulders. She leaned on her elbows, watching him pull off his own shirt. Reaching over, she ran a light hand over his fly. "Let me unwrap the package."

Julian knelt over her as she unzipped his pants, pulled them to his ankles, and then tugged at his briefs. His underwear gave way to reveal his throbbing, growing member.

Amber stroked his manhood gently, a lewd smile crossing her lips. She glowed with the heat of her own hungry body. Rising to her knees, she took him in her mouth, sucking deeply as her lips enclosed his foreskin. He groaned with undisguised pleasure as her lips caressed his hardness, making him fill her mouth with his masculinity and uniting her to him.

The microwave screeched, and Julian reluctantly drew away from Amber. He then raced to the finished dish. Amber turned onto her stomach. "Oh, come on! What in hell?"

"What indeed?" Julian removed the box, reached for a fork in the night table, and sampled the contents. Winking at her, he said simply, "I think you'll like this—once it cools down."

"What is it?" Amber crawled to the other side of the bed and reached for it. "I want it!" His smile sent a pleasurable shiver down her spine.

Julian held it out of reach and took another mouthful. "Bread pudding like my grandmother used to make, and I have plans for it."

"Yeah, I can see. You're eating it." Amber raised a quizzical eyebrow as she turned onto her side. "You don't want to share!" She pouted. "Didn't they teach you that in kindergarten?"

"We—well, I have other plans, too, and of course, I was taught all about sharing." Julian rested a knee on the bed. "I think you're adventurous enough, Ms. Librarian."

Amber grinned at him, rolled onto her back, and held out her arms. "Come to me. Do you want some kisses?"

Julian knelt on the bed, placed the box of pudding onto the end table, and then curled against Amber, stroking her bare breasts. The feel of his fingers against her skin sent a pleasurable tingle down her spine. She nuzzled against his arm and ran a lazy hand over his bare legs and then over his still erect member. He laughed and covered her mouth with burning lips, running a light hand over her stomach until he reached her womanhood. Lightly, his fingers caressed the recesses of her sex as his lips explored the soft flesh of her neck and cheeks.

Julian's lips lingered against her ear. He whispered, "I have something special planned for you and that pudding." Then, he caressed her most intimate parts, reaching inside her until ecstasy mounted within her. She purred under his touch while moving light fingers over his balls.

The feel of his fingers inside her sent waves of tingling excitement through her body. Every inch of her being vibrated with longing as her flesh turned to jelly under his touch.

He sighed with pleasure as she touched him. Slowly, with obvious longing, he placed a hot kiss on her lips, his tongue searching the innermost corners of her mouth. Then, with a lewd smile, he broke away and removed the box from the table. Reaching into it, he placed a hand inside the flaps and then held up a hand covered in pudding. With a grin, he smoothed it over her breasts.

Amber gasped as the warm, viscous pudding spread over her nipples and then her breasts. The sensation sent an electrical charge through her system. She giggled when he began sucking on her nipples and then slowly licking her breasts. She reached for his member, squeezing it gently. The warmth of his flesh vibrating inside her filled her whole being with a titillating delight. She giggled as he softly moaned under her touch.

"Oh, I have something else." Julian leaned on one elbow, giving her a slow, sexy smile before turning to the end table and removing a dark red rose.

"A rose?" Amber grinned, raising a quizzical eyebrow.

"Made of feathers." He laughed and ran it over her bare leg.

Amber laughed and snatched it from him. She ran it over his balls. He was already erect, waiting for her touch. "Can I play with the pudding?"

"My, my. My prim librarian wants to play! Of course, you may." He laughed, reached out, and lightly squeezed a nipple. "Are you my 'Dear Prudence' who wants to come out to play?"

Amber leaned over his body, feeling the delicious muscles clenched under her soft midsection. She reached into the plastic box, dabbed her fingers into the pudding and licked her finger. The delicious rum flavor slid down her throat. She reached for a raisin, put it in her mouth, then met his gaze, gave him her most knowing smile, and smeared the pudding onto his balls and cock.

"Do you want me to clean you off?"

Julian emitted a howling laugh. "Glad you let it cool down."

"I know how to make you happy." Amber tickled his balls before looming over him and taking him in her mouth. She sucked deeply, luxuriating in the swelling of his cock as well as the sweet, viscous taste of the rum-laced pudding. He gasped and moaned with pleasure under her body.

Then, skillfully, he turned her on her back and began spreading the pudding over her stomach and pubic mound. Laughing, he held up two raisins, raised his eyebrows, and then felt within the crevices of her vagina.

"You wouldn't!" Amber shrieked in lewd delight. What was she becoming? "Would you place food in such a place?"

"All the better to eat it, my dear!" He leered at her and then spread onto his stomach, letting his tongue reach into her sex.

Amber screamed with delight as his tongue tickled her most sensitive parts, sending desire-filled shivers through her entire being. Then, his hands moved inside her, bringing her to ecstasy. He kissed her thighs until they so relaxed that he loomed over her and straddled her body. He leaned into her, licking more of the pudding from her most scandalous parts as his member grew larger, harder. With a soft thrust, he was inside her, his manhood exploding. Never had she experienced this kind of sensation, of intimate connection.

\*\*\*

The next day, Amber clutched Julian's hand as they made their way to the Cliff House. Inside, they each ordered a Bloody Mary and shared multiple appetizers. It was there that Amber thought she saw a passing figure she knew all too well but quickly dismissed the possibility from her consciousness. Mary Stone had been carted away in New Orleans. The woman was no threat to her or her peace. Still, an uneasy foreboding seeped into her inner being.

The night before had been blissful, lying in Julian's arms after a luxurious shower together in a small but functional bathtub. They had lathered each other with soap, and God knew they needed it after smearing pudding all over their most intimate parts. They had washed each other's most intimate crevices and poured shampoo into each other's hair. Amber had giggled as he ran his hands through her hair, caressing her hair and face as he then licked her breasts while water cascaded down them both. She'd responded with soft caresses to his member until he grew hard, and then, he'd taken her again in the shower.

In the Cliff House, Amber sat beside Julian and clasped his hand as they fed each other. The salty Bloody Mary only made her crave water and the hardened muscles of the man beside her. "Do you really have to go back to base?"

Julian threw his head back and laughed. The gesture reminded Amber of Lucien, and a darkness settled over her soul. He answered lightly, "You aren't encouraging a soldier to desert his post, now are you, ma'am? Not a patriotic woman like you?"

"I'm just being selfish, Julian. I wish this time wouldn't end." Amber stared out of the windows—into the vastness of the ocean looming in the distance.

"It doesn't have to." Julian fiddled with his fork.

"What do you mean?"

"Marry me. We could do it in a few days. You wouldn't have to go back to my father and this weird situation you're in." Julian looked at her hard, forcing her to meet his gaze.

Amber felt the heat rush to her face. So he knew how depraved the relationship with Winston was. "Julian, this is a stolen time. You know that."

"Why can't you leave him?" Julian's hand closed over hers, hard.

"He needs me." Amber had never vocalized the words before. Why did she feel this way? In so many ways, Winston had her in his power, yet she pitied him. She swallowed hard. "Do you want me to hurt your father?"

"It's not that simple, and you know it. Winston's a loner. He has been since my mother died." Julian motioned to the waiter and ordered a whiskey. "Do you think you're the first woman to wear those outfits? Do you think you're the first young woman?"

A gasp escaped Amber's lips. "What do you know of—?"

"You're not the first."

Amber had known the truth of this statement for a long time, but the words were like cold ice over her whole body. She stammered. "I can't just desert him. You're going to deploy, and I know how he worries about you."

"Do you?" Julian's dark eyes bore into her.

"Yes, of course I do." Amber looked around, realizing how much she'd raised her voice. She drew closer to him, feeling the heat of his breath. Their foreheads touched. "You don't know how much of this is stolen time."

"It doesn't have to be stolen. We could marry. You'd be my wife and entitled to all benefits as well as information about me. You could stay here, leave the past behind you."

Amber sighed. *Why didn't she say yes? Why not run away with him?* She said simply, "We have two more days."

"So you'll think about it?"

"You know I will." She wanted to melt into his deep eyes. She sighed. "Still, there are some things you can't escape."

"Was your childhood happy?" Julian cast a penetrating glance in her direction.

The question startled Amber. She shrugged. "I guess. I mean, it was until my dad died. Life changed a lot for us after that." She hesitated and added, "Financially and socially."

"Well, I'm not sure if mine was ever too happy." He sipped his drink. "My parents were really volatile. They argued. I loved my mother, but she was pretty erratic. I don't think she ever liked that Dad became the really famous one. She'd wanted that for herself, but she loved me. I adored her, but the fighting between them was never fun. Then, they would act just fine together, kissing with arms around each other."

Amber stroked his hand. "I'm sorry. We don't have to talk about this."

Julian gave her hand a light squeeze. "Sometimes you need to talk about certain things." He flagged the waiter and ordered another drink. Turning back to her, he said, "My grandmother never liked my mother, my dad's mother. She raised me. Gran always said my dad should have married some other woman he'd met in college, but the woman had married his good friend."

A chill ran through Amber. "Oh, he had a good friend?" She tried to keep her voice casual.

Julian laughed softly. The waiter had brought him a whiskey on the rocks. He took a sip. "Yeah, at one time Winston Hurley actually had friends. I don't remember much about that time. I was eight when she died, and I've always had a mental blackout about that period."

Amber nodded. "So you don't remember those friends."

"My Gran just used to call the ex-girlfriend 'V.' " He ran a hand through his hair. "I guess it was a nickname."

Amber suddenly felt very cold. She cleared her throat. "Yeah, I guess so. Let's go back to the hotel. I'm feeling a little tired."

Julian's phone buzzed. He removed it from his pants pocket. "It's Winston. He's coming back to San Diego tomorrow."

Amber swallowed hard. "I told you it was stolen time."

"Think about what I said." Julian paid the check, stood, and took Amber's hand.

# Chapter Twelve

Amber watched as Julian pulled out the next day. She walked to Louie's, a breakfast shop frequented by locals and tourists alike. She sat at a corner table and opened a book, wondering when her life had become like that of some perverse romance novel. Gazing out at the fog spreading over the ocean and covering the landscape, Amber wrestled with a multitude of conflicting emotions.

In many ways, their brief time together had been perfect. Julian was handsome and the perfect lover—gentle yet skillful. Nonetheless, she couldn't deny the titillating yet toxic hold Winston had on her. In so many ways, she wanted Julian. Yes, Amber would marry him if his father weren't in the equation. But he was—and he drew her to him like a magnetic force. What the hell was wrong with her? Then, some of Julian's conversation about his parents was disturbing . . .

Then, Amber heard the voice. "I know you don't want to hear from me, but my information is something you'll want to hear."

Amber looked up, dread filling her whole soul. Mary Stone stood in front of her. "Ms. Stone, you're out of lock up. I'm glad you seem lucid."

"You're not the sweet little thing you pretend to be, are you?" Mary stared hard at her.

"I don't pretend anything. If people choose to see me a certain way, then that's their prerogative. I'm simply myself." Amber turned her attention to her book.

"You'll want to know—" The woman gripped the strap on her purse.

"If you become a nuisance, the San Francisco police will hear about your idiocy and your harassment. I don't think you'd like the inside of a San Francisco prison." Amber met her gaze. She kept her voice neutral as she sipped coffee. "Or the inside of a psych ward."

"Why are you here in San Francisco?" Mary gazed hard at her.

"I'm traveling. Seeing the sights." Amber bit into her toast. "I've always enjoyed San Francisco."

"Have you tracked down Terry Page?"

"Should I?" Amber sipped her coffee, looking at the woman over her cup.

"I think so. She lives here. You might find out some very interesting things if you converse with her." When Amber didn't respond, she added quickly, "Okay, I'll go, but she lives in the Haight." She scribbled something on a piece of paper and placed it on the table before turning on her heel.

Amber reached for the paper. It was a postcard with an address in the Haight quickly scribbled.

Amber was scheduled to leave for Austin the morning of New Year's Eve, but the day before, she sought out the address and phone number in the Haight. If Mary Stone had given her valid information in her search, she couldn't discard it. As the phone rang, Amber rehearsed what she would say to Terry Page. She identified herself as a freelance writer who was researching Lucien Travis and gave her last name as "Simmons."

Amber cleared her throat when the line connected. "Ms. Page, I'm Amber Simmons. I'm writing an article on Lucien Travis. I—I hope to sell it to a magazine, and I wondered if you'd talk to me."

There was a long pause on the other end of the line. Finally, Terry spoke. "Lucien's death was a dark time for me."

"I understand that, but his career is fascinating." Amber fought to keep her voice neutral as her heart pounded. Why in hell was she sweating? The answers to her questions would be as hard as not knowing.

"Well, I get that you want to make it in journalism." She paused. "Okay, I'll meet you at the Flywheel Café. Impeding a person's career isn't my thing, so I'll help you. We can talk about Lucien."

Amber arrived early at the coffee shop, ordered a coffee, and opened a newspaper. She glanced surreptitiously at passersby and other patrons. Finally, Terry entered the shop, looked around, nodded to Amber, and made her way to the counter. After retrieving her coffee, she stood before Amber with the mug in hand.

Amber indicated the chair opposite her. The woman before her was very different from the one she'd seen in pictures from her earlier days. Her once naturally blond hair now needed help from a bottle, but it was still marked by her trademark waves. Terry also still wore the flowing scarves and skirts Amber had noted in articles about the woman, but she no longer bore the svelte figure she'd once had. The ruddiness of her complexion showed that she drank more than she should.

"I'm not sure just what you want to know about Lucien Travis. He's long dead." Terry took a seat at the table opposite Amber. Her voice caught as she said the last words.

"Is he?" Amber stared at her over her mug. "There were rumors that he survived that car crash, that he even staged it."

"Those rumors were started by idiots—or fame-seekers." Terry sniffed derisively. "Too many conspiracy theorists exist."

"Well, it does seem tragic, his dying so soon after his wife. After all, their child was left parentless." Amber tried to keep her voice neutral as she removed a small notebook from her purse.

"Tragic it was, but Lucien's mother was a real presence. I'm sure she took care of the boy." Terry gave a muffled laugh. "The woman was a dynamo. If there had been a conspiracy, she would have been part of it. Supposedly, she made sure her preacher husband met his end."

Amber almost choked on her coffee. "Are you saying she killed him?"

"On record, he had a heart attack, but the old man was a tyrant. Lucien had some stories about him. Rumor has it he cheated, preacher though he was." Terry shrugged. "Who knows? It was a long time ago, but I'd met many of their friends from Texas. He was a mean bastard and a real fire-and-brimstone preacher. A hypocrite, though, in spite of all his piety. Supposedly, he had a woman. Lucien's mother, Ann, focused on him because there was no love in the marriage. Every woman he looked at had to face Ann's scrutiny, and none of them met her standards."

"So she didn't like Delta?"

"Couldn't stand her. Delta was from the wrong side of the tracks, so to speak." Terry folded her arms on the table. She nervously ran her tongue over her lips. "I wish I could have a cigarette. Of course, lighting up here anywhere is illegal. Fuck it!"

Amber studied the woman. She clearly was a shadow of her former self. What had so devastated her? She weighed the prudence of the next question and decided to take the gamble. Clearing her throat, she asked softly, "Were you one of his girlfriends?"

"I was in his college crowd, yeah, and when Lucien stung my heart, I never recovered."

"So what happened?" Amber leaned toward the woman, a fellow conspirator in girlfriend gossip.

"Well, Ann sure as hell didn't like me. I was too wild, she thought. Of course, she really hated Delta. Delta came after me." Terry looked down and grasped her cup. "She had no idea how wild Delta was—or Lucien, for that matter."

"So who ended it?" Amber sensed the woman would open up more if she seemed like some curious fan.

"Lucien had certain habits I didn't like. He was a good lover, but that was never enough for him. Then, he and his friend John met Vanessa. She was the perfect Louisiana magnolia. For a time, we drifted apart."

Amber's heart skipped a beat. She casually ran a hand through her hair and kept her voice neutral when she asked, "So you were all friends?"

"Well, it was a weird situation. I remained friends with them, but they were into games I didn't like. Vanessa eventually went to John. She always looked prim and proper, but that demeanor hid something else. Still, I think deep down she wanted that kind of stable life. John was more stable than Lucien in a lot of ways. Delta had wanted John at first, but she was too committed to music. Lucien was more her speed, but music never really happened for her."

Amber digested this. What didn't she know about her parents? "How did you become his manager?"

"I graduated with a business degree. Lucien contacted me and said he needed someone who'd studied music to handle his affairs. I had a minor in music even though I had no illusions about being a star. I admit that I liked the lifestyle, so I jumped at the opportunity."

"What happened the night Delta died?" Amber scribbled hurriedly in her notebook.

"I—I wasn't there." Terry picked up a spoon and began stirring her coffee. She produced a flask from her purse and poured the dark liquid into the cup. Amber detected a glimmer of fear in the woman's eyes. Her hands shook slightly.

"What happened to Lucien and Delta's son?" Amber continued to write in her notebook. Her mind was racing, and she wondered if her notes would even make sense later. She'd thought of taking a laptop, but decided against it. A laptop would freak out anyone.

"Ann had custody. Delta's parents were long dead, and Ann was the grandmother. She was from New Orleans, I think. She took him back there, couldn't wait to leave Texas and memories of her all-too-Christian husband." She took a sip from her cup. "The boy didn't speak after that night, that much I know. Lucien told me as much at Delta's funeral."

Amber took a deep breath. "What do you think happened?"

The woman shrugged. "Honestly, I think some of their games got out of hand. Personally, I don't think Delta's death was some accident, and that boy saw something really bad."

Amber shivered. What kind of mystery was she in? What role had her parents played in it? One thing she felt in her heart's core was that Lucien Travis was very much alive.

Amber arrived in Austin to learn that Vanessa had already returned to New Orleans. She sat in the living room with her grandmother the evening of her return, sipping coffee laced with a liberal shot of whiskey.

"How well did you know Lucien Travis?" she asked.

"He was John's best friend. He was always in my house while they were in college. They shared everything." Margaret sipped her coffee. The lights on the Christmas tree blinked behind her. She asked suddenly, "What is going on between you and this man you're 'house-sitting' for?" She made imaginary quotation marks around the word.

"Did he seem familiar to you?" Amber swallowed hard. What exactly was she looking for? "The man we met in Austin. He's the one."

"Familiar? In what way?" Margaret sighed. "So he's your boss, is he? More than that, I'll bet." She paused, as if considering and then shook her head. "The poor man was so scarred that I didn't think anyone could recognize the man he was."

Amber stared at her grandmother. "Gran, what are you saying? Do you know the man he was, as you say?"

"The man he seemed like is long dead. It's impossible, but he did play like Lucien. No one, not even my John, was quite like Lucien. The man had a real gift with the guitar, but he is dead many years. Dying so soon after his wife was tragic and suspicious, but people suffer double tragedies all the time. His mother collected all the insurance money and the son. She kept a low profile. We never saw them again."

Then, her voice caught. "Then, my John died. I understood Ann drifting off from other people. I didn't want to see anyone for the longest time after John died—very few people besides immediate family. With most people, though, they then move on and create a life. Ann dropped off the earth. Rumor had it she moved back to New Orleans and raised the boy."

Amber's heart skipped a beat. "So she stayed out of the public eye? Did you ever see the son?"

"Yes, but he was a handsome little boy, like his father. Of course, Delta was beautiful, too, and the boy was a sweet but mischievous kid. The funeral was very sad. The kid wasn't the same. He said nothing, just stood there like stone." Margaret took the coffee cups, refilling both with coffee and whiskey on the counter. "Lucien was very protective of the boy. He would have done anything to keep him safe. I think he was saying as much to your parents at the funeral. Then, of course, he died."

"Lucien was talking to my parents at the funeral?" Amber frowned and sipped the coffee.

"Yes, he said something in particular to them, like, 'We can never talk about this again.' "

"What did he mean?" Amber linked her hands together and leaned closer to her grandmother.

Margaret shrugged. "I don't know, honey. It was a long time ago. Besides, they stopped talking when I walked up. It was probably something old ladies shouldn't hear." She chuckled softly. "Like I'm some prim Southern belle." She sighed. "Well, I'm an old one, at any rate. I'm going to bed, darling." She stood and planted a kiss on Amber's forehead before heading to the door.

Amber stared after her grandmother. She wondered how much her grandmother knew and how much she was hiding because it seemed as if everyone was hiding something.

Amber returned to New Orleans the next day and retrieved Alwena from the groomer. They went to a beignet shop drive-up. Alwena and Amber always shared a treat when the dog boarded. Besides, Amber needed something to fortify her, body and soul. She had to talk to Vanessa, no matter how painful that would be. Her mother held the key to her past, and if she was to find any peace, Amber knew she had to penetrate the darkest secrets Vanessa held.

With the dog following at her heels, Amber emerged from her car and strode up the steps to her mother's front door. She inserted the key in the lock, not bothering to knock. Vanessa was home. Amber had seen her car.

"Well, how was your time in California? I wish we'd seen more of you in Texas." Vanessa met her in the hallway, placed a kiss on Amber's cheek, and then knelt to pet Alwena. The dog's tail thumped enthusiastically on the hardwood floor. Vanessa stood and met Amber's gaze. "I've missed you."

"I love you, Mama, but you've got to level with me." Amber's throat constricted. She wondered if trepidation would take her breath away.

"Don't tell me you're still thinking about Lucien." Vanessa led Amber into the kitchen. "He's long dead." She paused and retrieved two glasses from the cabinet. "Let's have some brandy."

"Yes, everyone seems to think he's dead." Amber sat across from Vanessa and took the glass her mother offered her.

"But you don't?" Vanessa arched an eyebrow and sipped from her glass.

Amber voiced the suspicions she'd never said aloud. "No, I think he's the man I've been living with." She took a deep breath and stared at her mother.

"And he's the guitarist we met in Austin." When Amber didn't respond and looked away, Vanessa persisted. "Am I wrong?"

"No, you're not." Amber's voice rang out, too shrill in her own ears.

"I'm guessing your relationship isn't platonic, is it?"

Amber stole a glance at Alwena. The dog lay placidly at her feet, but she shot what looked like a cynical look in Amber's direction. Amber answered evenly, "No, it's not platonic."

"I see." Vanessa folded her arms and rested her elbows on the table. "And you think you've been sleeping with some kind of ghost. If this is Lucien, how would he have pulled this charade off for so long?"

Amber spread her hands wide. "I don't know, but you have to tell me what you saw that night."

"Why? Why can't you let the past stay buried?" Vanessa sighed heavily, a sob escaping from her lips.

"Because I'm in love with his son!" With shaking hands, Amber took a sip of the brandy.

"Sweet Jesus, what kind of bizarre thing are you into?" Vanessa stared at her in horror.

"Mama, you don't want to know." Amber clutched the glass until her fingers were white.

"I probably don't want to know, but I must know. What have you done with this young man?"

"Let's just say we know each other in the biblical sense." Amber laughed dryly. When she saw her mother's eyes fill with tears, she said quickly, "I'm sorry, Mama. I am, but what happened that weekend? What do you know?"

"*I don't know anything.*" Vanessa bit her lip. "I didn't see Delta fall, but Lucien was standing over her when John and I heard Lucien give this strangled cry. We came running, and Justin was standing at the top of the stairs. Lucien was at the bottom by Delta." Vanessa's voice caught. She looked away. "You—you could see her neck was broken."

A bird chirped outside. Amber took a sip of her wine and stared at Vanessa over her glass. Her voice came out in a whisper and caught as her heart thundered inside of her. "Where were you and Daddy before she fell? Tell me, Mama, what kind of a visit was it?"

Vanessa sighed. She reached across the table and clutched Amber's hand. "I—I was with Lucien. Your father was with Delta."

"In the biblical sense?" Amber laughed dryly. "That's the dirty little secret that linked your high school/college friends together, isn't it?" She pulled her hand away. "You all liked it kinky."

Vanessa's face crumpled as tears rolled down her face. "We were all saying goodbye. All of us knew what we were doing wasn't right. You were so little. Justin was a little older but not much. We agreed never to see each other again. It was all for you and Justin. Then, Lucien and I heard Vanessa running for the stairs. He ran out the room."

"Why?" Amber's voice sounded shrill in her own ears.

"I'm not sure. John later said he thought someone was in the hall while he was with Vanessa, but Lucien was with me. He didn't leave until he heard her footsteps pounding down the hall. There was a scream. I threw on some clothes, and then, John and I saw her at the bottom of the stairs. Justin was staring, like someone in shock. Lucien bolted up the stairs, grabbed Justin by the arm, and pulled him into his room. He told us to go."

"And you did? With no question?" Amber shook her head.

"We didn't want the publicity. Your father had his business by then. Delta was in a slip when I saw her at the bottom of the stairs. The pictures I saw later didn't show her in a slip. Lucien must have changed her clothes. He didn't want anyone to know what had happened, either."

"Did he push her?" Amber's throat grew tight. Her fingers tightened around the stem of the glass.

Vanessa shook her head. She managed a slight laugh. "Why would he? I have no idea what happened, and then, Lucien died. His mother then disappeared with the child."

"Mama." Amber's voice was soft. She reached for Vanessa' s hand. "Mama, is Winston Hurley Lucien Travis?"

Vanessa covered her face with her hands, resting her elbows on the table. She looked up and brushed the hair from her face. "It's impossible. How could it be? Just leave him alone—both of  them."

# Chapter Thirteen

"I need to see you." Amber clutched her cell tightly when Julian answered. She sat cross-legged on the bed in her old room. It was strange living back in her mother's house after spending so much time in Winston Hurley's lush French Quarter home, but Amber couldn't return to him. To do so would be to betray her own conscience; as of yet, she didn't have to face Winston or explain her behavior. He was still playing the traveling minstrel.

"I'd love to see you, too, darling, but I can't get away from base until New Year's. I can manage a day or two then." There was a long pause. "Have you thought about my proposition?"

Amber ran a hand through her hair and laughed nervously. "You do realize what you're asking, don't you? We're betraying your father. Does that bother you? It bothers me."

Julian sighed deeply over the phone. "Of course, but you have to understand something. My father has played this game before. There have been other girls, Amber. You're not the first who has played this game with him. There will be others."

"I still need to talk to you." Amber swallowed and took a breath. "I have to know about the past."

"I'll see you New Year's Eve." Julian paused for a long time. "I love you. Don't let me down on this. I'll see you in Biloxi at New Year's. There's a meeting I have to attend in Mississippi. We can meet at the Hard Rock." Without another word, he hung up.

Alwena jumped onto the bed and nudged Amber's arm. Amber clutched the dog against her. "Well, you love me, don't you?" She buried her face in the dog's fur. "Girl, sometimes I think I'm about to open a bomb." Alwena's paw thumped against the bedspread. She licked Amber's arm as Amber wept softly.

Amber saw Trish as she made her way through a mall in a New Orleans suburb. She was shopping for her getaway with Julian. Or was he Julian? If Winston Hurley was indeed Lucien Travis, then Julian wasn't Julian. He was Justin, the long-lost son caught in a web of intrigue and deception. What did he know of his father's death? His mother's? Was he a willing or unwilling pawn in this bizarre game Winston/Lucien was playing?

Amber pushed those thoughts from her mind as the woman who'd upset her world came into view. Trish approached from the opposite direction, a shopping bag clutched tightly. Of all the people to ruin her day! Trish was walking immediately in her direction, but she apparently didn't see Amber. *Clearly, the bitch would scamper to the other side of the mall if she'd seen me,* Amber thought. *Besides, why isn't she in prison?* Before Amber could duck into a store, Trish was upon her. Amber met her gaze only to see that Trish's were filled with tears.

"I guess you're feeling a lot of joy right now." Trish's lip trembled. "You ruined me, and now, you've taken my child." Trish's voice reached a shrill pitch.

"What in hell do you mean?" Amber looked around her. Shoppers passed them in the aisle and glanced their way.

"My—my son is going into the marines. He would have gone in after college as an officer. Now, he's a recruit, and when he finishes, he's going to some godawful place like Afghanistan." Trish took a deep breath in an obvious attempt to control her emotions. Her fingers wrapped around the handle on the bag she held. "I—I have plans for my son, but now, we can't afford them since I have no job and am under indictment. My own trial starts in a month. I could be in jail soon. I hope you got what you wanted."

Amber stared at her. "I have nothing against your son, Trish. He was always polite to adults even though I'd heard he was a"—she made quotation marks in the air—"a 'blow job king' with the female student population. Regardless, he's not doing anything than a lot of young people haven't done before. Many of my male relatives went into the military as enlisted men. They weren't rich. They had no connections. Why should your son be any different?" She lowered her voice to a vicious whisper. "And if you did to the troops you should have protected, you should have the death penalty."

"How dare you?" Trish looked at the passersby staring her way and darted into the food cart. She glared at Amber, her voice a deadly whisper. She waved her arms in the air. "I know you were somehow responsible for what happened to me. I don't know how, but I just know."

Amber moved to Trish. She glanced around as a crowd gathered. A security officer made his way to the growing scene. "You brought your own problems on yourself. You're a traitor. You should be tried and sentenced to hell. I only pray for your son's sake that no one betrays his unit the way you betrayed your fellow soldiers when you were supposed to be serving. You're a traitor!"

"Everything okay, ladies?" The mall cop looked like a middle school kid. His stare moved between the two women as he nervously fingered his radio.

"All's well, officer, but this lady is a danger to national security." Amber turned to go.

Before Amber could go, Trish said through gritted teeth, "You got what you wanted. You won." Trish wiped a tear that escaped from her eyes.

"I didn't plan to win. You set me up with Tyler. You enjoyed watching me fail. I did you nothing, but you hated me." Amber looked at her hard. "You have no more power over me." With that, she turned on her heel.

The young guard wiped a blond lock into his cap. His Adam's apple bulged as he said, "I think you ladies should leave."

"I'm telling you I love her, and I don't want you getting in the way. I'll only get this opportunity once in a lifetime." Julian's voice broke. "But I'm scared. There's so much I don't remember. So much I don't understand." Julian clutched the phone hard in his hand as he paced the deserted room in the barracks.

"Those times are best forgotten." Winston's voice echoed through the phone. "You've been well for years. Don't do anything to unsettle the progress you've made. An affair like this could hurt your health."

"It's not fair what you're doing to her." Julian could hear his father's heavy breathing over the phone.

"Don't be ridiculous. I can keep you both safe and happy."

Julian's throat went dry. "I'm not going to share her. She's not what you've had in the past. She's special."

"Maybe so, but I don't want you hurt." Winston's voice crackled on the other line. "It took years for you to not have nightmares."

"You were never honest about why I had them. Whenever I got close to the truth with any therapist, Gran would make sure I saw someone else." Julian lowered his voice. "What were you afraid of?"

"It wasn't fear. You didn't need to know everything about your mother's death. You just didn't." Winston's voice rose to a fevered pitch.

"Why? Did you kill her?" Julian glanced around as he said the words.

Julian's bunkmate entered clad in military-issued shorts, rubbing his wet hair with a towel. He said quickly, "I think my hair needs more drying." With that, he ducked out the door.

"Dad?" The phone had gone dead. Julian sat on the bed and buried his face in his hands. He wept. How could he be worthy of Amber with so much unanswered?

### Two days later

"I love you."

Amber gazed into Julian's eyes when he opened the door to his room at Hard Rock. She felt her insides melt into a warm liquid. "I love you, too. I've never felt this way." She swallowed hard. "I'm sorry for how we met, but I'm not sorry we did."

Julian encircled her in his arms and drew her into the room. He pushed in her one bag and slammed the door. Classic rock videos played on the screen as he locked her in a kiss that wrapped her soul in mind-consuming ecstasy. He lifted her and moved with her to the bed.

Amber giggled as she fumbled with his belt buckle and then the button on his jeans. She produced a feather shaped like a rose from her purse, threw the bag onto the floor, and ran the feather along his face and neck. Julian ran his hand along her sweater dress, tickling her stomach and then her breasts before tugging at the dress and pulling it over her arms. He grinned at her as he sucked her nipples and then ran a warm tongue over her breasts and stomach. Amber tugged at his pants and briefs, exposing his bulging member. She rose to her knees to help him push his shirt off his shoulders and see it pool onto the bed. Their lips locked in hot desire as their skin touched. Julian ran a hand along her stomach and pushed her panties down her legs. Amber laughed and lay onto the bed, kicking her legs while Julian pulled the lace garment from her, tossing it onto the floor.

Amber stroked Julian's member with one hand and his balls with the other as he loomed over her. He bent over her, kissing her calves and then her thighs until she spread them effortlessly. She then sat upright and sucked on his manhood until he grew like a beacon inside her mouth while he stroked her wet, welcoming womanhood.

After she'd wet his already pulsing body gun, Amber fell onto her back. Julian nibbled on her neck as he covered her with his body. He exploded inside her, filling her whole body with shivering ecstasy as their bodies went rigid. As he released his maleness, Julian rested against her, his body wet.

Amber and Julian slept as the music played; they showered and then ordered drinks and food from room service. They drank wine and ate cheese as music videos played on the television screen.

It was as they finished a bottle of red wine that a video of the young Lucien Travis flashed onto the screen. Amber froze as she watched it, her insides turning to liquid as doubts and fears cascaded through her brain. Julian, too, seemed frozen, a glass of wine at his lips.

"Who are you? Really? What do you remember?" Amber met his gaze and began to shake. Why hadn't she seen it before?

The man calling himself Winston Hurley handed his keys to the valet at the hotel and made his way into the lobby, ascended the staircase, and checked into the room he'd booked for his brief stay. He knew the room where his son would stay; the kid was a creature of habit. The room where he was cavorting with Amber was the same one he'd stayed in with Winston on his gigs here. Not that Julian suspected the truth. There were gaps in his memory, and Winston was determined to make certain the gaps remained. No one would benefit if Julian's memory returned. He checked the small, leather overnight bag he carried. The gun was stored safely in the holster. Yes, he would need it later.

"What do you mean? What does it matter?"

Amber sat up and stared hard at Julian. "I'm so stupid. I'm just seeing how much like Lucien Travis you are."

"It doesn't matter. It was a different life, and there's a lot I don't remember." Julian stood at the side of the bed and pushed into his shirt and pants. "All I know is my dad knew we had to disappear."

"Did he kill your mother?" Amber let the sheets drop around her waist. She hugged her bare breasts and shivered. Her voice was a shrill cry; her mouth went dry.

It was then they heard the knock on the door. Amber reached for her dress and pulled it over her head.

Julian met her gaze and then moved to the door. He sighed deeply before saying, "Sorry! We didn't mean to make too much noise."

"Open up, kid!"

Amber gasped, feeling the breath almost leave her body. How had Winston/Lucien found them? Her gaze flew to Julian's. "Did you tell him we were here?"

"No, I—I—" Julian stuttered, but the pounding intensified. He threw the door open with one thrust.

Winston stood before them, a genial smile on his scarred face. "May I come in?"

Amber stood at the side of the bed, frozen. A hard realization enveloped her, almost making her knees buckle. *How had she missed it? Why had she ever doubted?* The man standing before them in jeans and cowboy hat could be none other than Lucien Travis. Scarred he may be, but every gesture he made was clearly the man she'd studied in videos. What game was he playing? What game was Julian playing? She finally swallowed, willing saliva into her mouth.

"How long have you known about us?"

"Darling, I'm not a stupid man. I may be a little bit of a red neck, but Texans aren't dumb cowboys." His grin widened. He stepped past his son and stared from Amber to Julian. His gaze rested on Julian. "I only wanted to protect you. That's all."

Amber hugged her midsection. She wanted to run from the room, find shelter somewhere else, but she stared at Julian as tears cascaded down her cheeks. She couldn't run—no matter what happened. She loved him too much to run.

Finally, she drew air into her lungs. "Did you kill Delta? Did my mother? My father?"

Julian gazed at her, a puzzled expression on his face. "What the fuck—?"

Winston grinned and laughed dryly. He slipped his hands into his pockets. "I never thought I'd see your mother again, but then here she came walking into a club with a pretty girl a lot like her." He paused, moved to the refrigerator in the room and removed a bottle of whiskey. "I know my boy. I know where he keeps his liquor." He winked at Amber and poured the golden liquid into glasses atop the dresser.

He crossed to Amber and handed her a glass. Amber saw that his hand trembled as he held it. Then, he moved to his son and handed the glass to him. When he took his own glass, he lifted it in a toast. "Here's to family reunions."

With a hard look at Amber, he said, "I hope you realize what kind of can you just opened. This ain't no worms, darling." He downed the drink with one swallow.

"Dad, look, I love her!" Julian's voice held desperation. "We didn't mean to sneak around behind your back."

"Well, I hope she's worth jeopardizing the secret we kept all these years." Winston hurled the glass onto the wall. It shattered at his feet. He looked at Amber. "I don't think you see the kind of psyche you risk hurting."

"I've told her nothing. I know what happened to Mama was an accident. I know you didn't mean to and that's why we had to leave." Julian's eyes had misted over as he spoke. His voice caught.

The scarred man studied his son. "You really don't remember, do you? Even yet?" He laughed softly, without mirth, and shook his head. "I did it all to protect you—crashed the car, damaged myself, all so that I could disappear and your grandmother could claim the inheritance and control it for us. I made sure the scars were so bad that nobody would recognize me. Playing still drove me, and I could do it with your grandmother watching you while I lived like a gypsy."

Julian downed his own drink. His fingers closed so tightly around the glass that Amber thought it would break. "What the fuck do you mean? I saw you at the top of the stairs."

Amber climbed across the bed to stand by Julian. She didn't want to risk even touching Winston. What in hell game was he playing? She winced inwardly. What crazy game had she played for so long? Gently, she placed a hand on Julian's shoulder.

"What did you do to Delta?"

"We were ending our little game with John and Vanessa. They wanted it over, too. We knew that kind of crap couldn't go on with you kids." He ran a hand over his face. "It was only supposed to be a goodbye. Nobody was supposed to walk in." He stared hard at Julian. "You weren't supposed to come home that night, but you were getting sick. Your grandmother needed the medicine your mother kept for you." His voice caught. "Why the fuck did you go to that bedroom?"

A light flickered in Julian's eyes. A dawning realization seemed to hit him slowly. He lunged at Winston, clutching his father's collar, and bellowed, "Jesus! She was in bed with him, not you! I ran from there!"

His voice cracked. Tears suddenly escaped from his eyes. Winston gathered him in his arms and pushed him into the chair beside the bed.

"I screamed for you! I yelled for Grandma, then Mama was running after me!" Julian's eyes widened in terror! "Oh, shit! She grabbed me! I pushed her away! She made to grab at me again, and I was fighting. That's when she scratched my chin." He buried his face in his hands. His weeping became a hollow. "I didn't mean for her to fall! Oh, Christ, I didn't mean for her to fall!" He clutched the bedsheets in a tight fist.

Amber reached for him even as she trembled. The horror of his realization hit her like a body blow. Her breath deserted her even as she clung to his shoulders. Drawing in her breath, she whispered, "It wasn't your fault, Julian."

Winston moved closer to his son. "No, it wasn't your fault. You were in shock, and after that night, you never spoke for a long time." He gingerly touched his son's shoulder. "I couldn't let them ever become suspicious. The police questioned me. They suspected me, not you. John and Vanessa—well, shit, I didn't know how much they actually saw or suspected. Vanessa had been on my heels when I ran to find you. I had heard you and was running out of the bedroom when I saw what happened. You were pushing her away from you. You couldn't have known she'd lose her balance and fall. You'd obviously blocked out the whole thing." Winston glared at Amber. "It took him years of therapy, and he never remembered until now."

"I never meant for her to fall! I just didn't want her to touch me! What I saw disgusted me!" Julian slumped into Amber's arms.

Winston touched his arm. "I know you didn't, but I couldn't risk them ever finding us. They suspected me, but I couldn't let them get near you. Your mental health was fragile."

Amber hugged her midsection. The whole thing made her feel sick. "So you crashed the car on purpose. "

"Yes, darling. I knew a doctor and lawyer of questionable repute. One drafted new identities for me. Another did this job on my face. I couldn't be famous anymore, but it didn't matter." He pulled a chair near and sat beside Julian, running a hand through his hair. "It was to protect you. So you became Julian. I became Winston. Your grandmother used the name Hurley, her maiden name." He stroked Julian's arm. "It was worth becoming the traveling minstrel to keep you safe. I only regret you found out later about the women I had."

"I killed her. I killed her." Julian touched his father's arm, gazing up at him as tears stained his face.

"You DIDN'T! We did this ourselves with our greed and insanity. You were an innocent bystander."

"So we've lived a lie!" Julian shook his head and laughed dryly.

"It was a lie for love, Julian." Amber found her voice. The anger she thought she would feel died before it was born. She could feel no animosity toward Winston or her parents. Hell, weren't we all flawed? Still, she felt like an actor in a game, a pawn in a chess game over which she'd had no control. She ran a hand over her hair, suddenly aware of how disheveled she was. Still, she hated being used. "Why did you single me out? You saw my mother. I could tell she sensed something about you. Did you do it for some kind of revenge?"

"No, darling, you were just beautiful. You were Vanessa all those years ago. And you were like John, generous and kind. You brought me back to that other time. I'd wanted a time back when my life had included all that love—love of my best friend and love of two women." He touched Julian's hair. "I didn't love anyone like I'd loved your mother, and she loved me, too. What we'd enjoyed with other people was the thrill of sex and the hint of scandal. It was adventure, and we were safe with each other. We never thought you"—he turned to Amber—"or you would find out what we'd done. I just couldn't resist you, darling, but I'm going to release you with no qualms."

Amber arched an eyebrow. A sliver of ire raced down her spine. "I wasn't yours to release."

Julian ran the back of his hand over Amber's face and then closed his hand over hers. "She's mine."

"I'm not disputing it, but she also has to be herself. What I had with her was only a lost dream, a stolen glimpse into a past I can't reinvent." Winston lightly touched Amber's cheek. "So beautiful but so sensual, and it couldn't last. I only hope you two can forget the past."

A shiver ran through Amber's whole being. Could they rise above a past that all-consuming and destructive? Could they forge a life? A family? Amber bit her lip so hard it bled. "I—I don't know where this is going." She turned to Julian. No matter what, her destiny was linked to his. She steeled herself and said with resolve. "I'll help you. We'll get through this."

"Yes, you will, but there's no need for me to stay." Winston quickly wrapped his son in his arms, planting a rough kiss on the top of Julian's head. Julian initially wrestled against the strong embrace but then collapsed against his father as the sobs subsided.

After a long time, Winston released Julian. He stood, tipped his hat to Amber, and said, "Goodbye, darling. Take care of each other." With that, he turned on his heel and opened the door.

Julian held Amber tight, whispering in her ear. "I love you. Don't leave me. We can work out whatever this crazy legacy is." His voice grew desperate. "I can't live without you."

Amber melted into his arms, her own doubts vanishing in his hot embrace. "I won't leave you."

Two weeks later, the newscaster's voice droned on with some excitement:

*Presumed dead musician Lucien Travis is at the center of a baffling and complex mystery! Apparently, the car crash that allegedly killed the man in the 1990s was staged to enable Travis's disappearance from the performing world. The body of Lucien Travis has recently been found in a New York City hotel— over twenty years after the supposed crash that killed the guitarist. He was the victim of a gunshot wound. This news has taken the music world by storm. . .*

The attorney sat across from Julian and Amber. He tapped a file on his massive mahogany desk. A picture of a leggy, dark-haired beauty adorned the desk. Clearing his throat, he said, "I was your father's trustee many years ago, and I still am. He's left you a sizable legacy."

"But there was fraud." Julian's hand closed over Amber's. "Will we be held responsible for fraud?"

George Pfister, the attorney, shrugged. He was a tall, athletic man with fair hair and a very polished Southern accent. "Technically, there was no fraud. Your grandmother cashed an insurance policy. She supposedly didn't know whether or not your father was dead. There was no law against your father wanting to retire from the limelight. His changing your name and his was a way of maintaining privacy. Leaving other people guessing about what happened to him wasn't illegal. He didn't kill anyone to crash that car. He simply changed his name and worked for pennies. As for the car crash, well, maybe he left it confused and didn't report it." He discreetly coughed. "Of course, this time, the authorities can't prove suicide, so your father's fortune, including the insurance policy, have grown."

Amber looked at Julian. He clearly was absorbing what he'd heard. Amber turned to the lawyer. "If Winston, or Lucien, was playing for peanuts, how did this fortune grow?"

"Investments. Lucien was very shrewd, not some cracker. Besides, his mother was also one smart woman. She was frugal and made her own investments. They have fallen to him and then to Julian." He looked at Julian. "The question for you is will you become Justin again or remain Julian."

Julian ran a hand over his chin. "I'm a Travis. Julian was my middle name. That's why my dad decided to use it." He'd begun to remember many things about his past, and those memories softened the anger the initial revelation had kindled. He raised Amber's hand to his lips. "We can start over. The money is our chance. We can open the business you always talked about."

Amber laughed happily at his optimism. "You won't leave the military."

"Maybe not, but we have options. Besides, you can travel to every post with me and not worry." Julian continued. "I've paid my respects to dad. He's lying in his mother's family tomb in New Orleans. He's at rest, at least I hope he is." He looked from Amber to the lawyer and then back at Amber. "He was always such a shadowy figure. I was never sure he loved me. Now, I know he did, and he was willing to sacrifice himself for me." His voice fell to a whisper. "I wish he hadn't felt the need to do that."

Amber swallowed hard. She'd harbored so many mixed emotions for the man who had introduced her to many taboo but thrilling forms of love and lust. "He was always protecting you. Poor Lucien. Living with that secret mustn't have been easy."

Pfister reached into a desk drawer. "Ms. Thorpe, he also left you a letter."

Amber's eyes widened in surprise. She took it gingerly, as if the contents would explode in her hand. She would read it later—much later.

# Chapter Fourteen

"So you are sure you want to keep the house—even with the memories?" Julian looked over his shoulder at Amber as they made their way into the French Quarter home carrying boxes. Alwena pushed ahead of them, tail wagging, and made her way to the kitchen where a bowl of treats already awaited her.

"Are you certain before we carry this stuff in?"

"Yes, the house is gorgeous. Besides, you've said you were happy here with your grandmother after your mother died. When and if you leave the military, we can come back here. We just have to make it ours. If you deploy, I'll stay here and make it home for you. For you and the many babies we'll make together."

To that end, Amber had purchased new fixtures and decorations for the house. Pictures of her family as well as Julian's graced the walls. She placed a box on a waiting table after Julian opened the door. "We will get a new bed."

Julian met her gaze. An amused flicker lit his eyes. "Yes, I think that's in order." He placed his own box beside hers and opened it, adding softly, "Your mother has called, by the way."

"Do you mind if she comes to the wedding? I mean, it's going to be with a justice of the peace, but I'd like some of my closest people there."

Amber had grappled with her mother's role in the whole Travis affair, but this was a happy time for them. Maybe Vanessa had wanted to protect her just as Lucien had wanted to protect his son. Amber and Vanessa had been close too long to lose that relationship, even though Amber still held some reservations about her mother's trustworthiness.

"Of course, she's invited. What would this be like without your

Gran or your mother?" He laughed. "Even some of the old rock crowd has contacted me. It may be good to have them. They're mainly curious about the whole situation with Dad,
but—"

He paused.

"After all, you've decided to write. It may be good for your career to have influential people around."

Amber smiled up at him. "Your father wasn't the only savvy one. Yeah, I think a wedding in a hall with a few close people would be nice. Just don't make this a Mick and Bianca wedding, my love."

Julian laughed without reservation this time and planted a kiss on her lips. "You have my word that McCartney won't be there."

"Well, he is pretty influential. Maybe he'll proofread my book."

"I'll proofread your book and every other part of you!" Julian placed a smoldering kiss on her lips that turned her legs to liquid blues.

"Maybe we can finish the unpacking later." Amber's voice was choked with passion as she smiled at him.

The End

# About the Author

Viola Russell is the pseudonym for Susan Weaver Eble. A homegrown New Orleanian, she holds a doctorate in English Literature from Texas A & M University. She has travelled far and wide and relishes the memories she has made in places as distant as England, Ireland, Canada, and Jamaica and as near as Mississippi, Texas, Oklahoma, California, and Massachusetts. She lives with her husband Ben, the love of her life, in a New Orleans cottage and is most comfortable at her computer creating the worlds that drift into her imagination.

## More Black Velvet Seductions titles

Their Lady Gloriana by Starla Kaye
Cowboys in Charge by Starla Kaye
Her Cowboy's Way by Starla Kaye
Punished by Richard Savage, Nadia Nautalia & Starla Kaye
Accidental Affair by Leslie McKelvey
Right Place, Right Time by Leslie McKelvey
Her Sister's Keeper by Leslie McKelvey
Playing for Keeps by Glenda Horsfall
Playing By His Rules by Glenda Horsfall
The Stir of Echo by Susan Gabriel
Rally Fever by Crea Jones
Behind The Clouds by Jan Selbourne
Trusting Love Again by Starla Kaye
Runaway Heart by Leslie McKelvey
The Otherling by Heather M. Walker
First Submission - Anthology
These Eyes So Green by Deborah Kelsey
Dark Awakening by Karlene Cameron
The Reclaiming of Charlotte Moss by Heather M. Walker
Ryann's Revenge by Rai Karr & Breanna Hayse
The Postman's Daughter by Sally Anne Palmer
Final Kill by Leslie McKelvey
Killer Secrets by Zia Westfield
Crossover, Texas by Freia Hooper-Bradford
The King's Blade by L.J. Dare
Uniform Desire - Anthology
Safe by Keren Hughes
Finishing the Game by M.K. Smith
Out of the Shadows by Gabriella Hewitt
A Woman's Secret by C.L. Koch
Her Lover's Face by Patricia Elliott
Love Times Infinity by K.L. Ramsey
Naval Maneuvers by Dee S. Knight
Love's Patient Journey by K.L. Ramsey
Perilous Love by Jan Selbourne
Patrick by Callie Carmen
Love's Design by K.L. Ramsey

The Brute and I by Suzanne Smith
Love's Promise by K.L. Ramsey
Home by Keren Hughes
Worth the Wait by K.L. Ramsey
Only A Good Man Will Do by Dee S. Knight
Secret Santa by Keren Hughes
The Christmas Wedding by K.L. Ramsey
Killer Lies by Zia Westfield
A Merman's Choice by Alice Renaud
Theirs to Keep by K.L. Ramsey
Line of Fire by K.L. Ramsey
Theirs to Love by K.L. Ramsey
All She Ever Needed by Lora Logan
Nicolas by Callie Carmen
Torn Devotion by K.L. Ramsey
The Story of JESS & AVER by K.A. Neeson
Theirs to Have by K.L. Ramsey
Fighting for Justice by K.L. Ramsey
Paging Dr. Turov by Gibby Campbell
Theirs to Take by K.L. Ramsey
Out of the Ashes by Keren Hughes
A Thread of Sand by Alan Souter
Stolen Beauty by Piper St. James
Mystic Desire anthology
Killer Deceptions by Zia Westfield
Edgeplay by Lora Logan
Music for a Merman by Alice Renaud
Joseph by Callie Carmen
Not You Again! By Patricia Elliott

Our back catalog is being released on Kindle Unlimited
You can find us on:
Twitter: BVSBooks
Facebook: Black Velvet Seductions
See our bookshelf on Amazon now! Search "BVS Black Velvet
Seductions Publishing Company"

*Black Velvet Seductions*

www.ingramcontent.com/pod-product-compliance
Lightning Source LLC
Chambersburg PA
CBHW030626130626
46552CB00002B/719